LAST WORDS

ALSO BY INES SAINT

Angie Gomez Cozy Murder Mystery Series

Last Words

Word Games

Fun Contemporary Romances

The Politics of Love

Charmed

LAST WORDS

ANGIE GOMEZ COZY MURDER MYSTERY, BOOK 1

INES SAINT

Edited by

IMBUE EDITING

Book and cover design by eBook Prep
www.ebookprep.com

June, 2021
ISBN: 978-1-64457-226-9

ePublishing Works!
644 Shrewsbury Commons Ave
Ste 249
Shrewsbury PA 17361
United States of America

www.epublishingworks.com
Phone: 866-846-5123

A special thanks to Tomás Ruiz for all the cultural knowledge and fun conversations about our heritage, which will eventually wind their way into the series. I named the ship after you!

ANGIE'S UNOFFICIAL ABRIDGED SPANISH AND PUERTO RICAN SPANISH/ENGLISH DICTIONARY

abuela: grandmother
abuelo: grandfather
bioco: conniption
Briscas: Spanish playing cards
chismear: gossip
mija: combination of "mi" (my) and (hija) daughter; an affectionate term, not always an endearment
nena: girl
no tientes: don't tempt
telenovela: soap opera (in Latin America, typically last three months to a year)
tirada rápida: quick card reading
tostones: fried plantains
¿que te pasa?: What's wrong with you? or What's going on with you?

PROLOGUE

"When life itself seems lunatic, who knows where madness lies? Perhaps to be too practical is madness. To surrender dreams —this may be madness. Too much sanity may be madness—and maddest of all: to see life as it is, and not as it should be!"

MIGUEL CERVANTES SAAVEDRA,
DON QUIXOTE

"The three-card spread is for cowards, Angie," Abuela Luci grumbled as she held the deck of Spanish Brisca cards out to me. It was late, and her last client had canceled. I was a poor substitute when it came to fortune-telling (my reactions weren't dramatic enough for my grandmother), but we were both bored. "A horseshoe spread would give you more answers."

"Next time. I promise." I chose three cards and laid them, left to right, on the time-worn mahogany table.

"Turn them over, one by one," she instructed as if I were doing this for the first time.

I turned over the first card and glanced up.

"Seven of coins," Abuela said on a gasp. "Turn over the next one." I did as I was told. "*Tres de bastos*! Three of clubs," she exclaimed, nodding excitedly. "The last one, Angie. Turn it over. Now."

"Nine of clubs," I said as I laid the last card down.

Abuela grabbed my hands, her eyes shimmering with excitement. I didn't believe in fortune-telling or magic, but I smiled in anticipation all the same. My grandmother was the most perceptive woman I knew, and there was always wisdom when she spoke to me about my life and choices.

"Many changes are coming your way, Angie. A stagnant matter will begin to move along. It all starts with a change in your professional circumstances and a new discovery about yourself."

If only I could believe her. I was a sculptor who could only find paid work making busts of local prominent figures, both current and historic. What possible change in professional circumstances or personal discovery could help move the only stagnant matter I cared about: my parents' unsolved murder?

Abuela met my eyes. "Believe, Angie."

She raised an eyebrow. "You managed to get a meeting with him so soon?"

"Not quite. But he'll see me." I gave her the mischievous smile she said reminded her of my dad.

Abuela winked. "That's my girl."

ONE

"Plow with the oxen you've got."

PUERTO RICAN PROVERB, AS
TRANSLATED BY ABUELA LUCI

"I'm sorry, but Lieutenant Mahoney is in back-to-back meetings today," the new deputy informed me, his voice laced with regret. "If you show me some identification, I'll be happy to make an appointment for you to see him later." The nameplate pinned to his crisp dark green shirt read Corporal Benny Rover. Snub nose, long face, prominent upper chest, and a head full of golden-orange fuzz. Trying hard to look busy but holding himself tense. Likely a deputy fresh out of the academy who imagined he was being watched and didn't want to make mistakes. No doubt, it was why he'd been chosen to guard the new major crimes unit supervisor from people like me.

"Who is he meeting with right now?" I asked as I handed him my driver's license.

"Uh..." The young corporal looked around to see if anyone was close enough to guide him. No one was. "He's meeting with Captain Webber, I believe."

"Excellent! He'll want to see me, too," I bluffed. "Let them know I'm here. There's no need to make an appointment for later."

"Right. Angie Gomez Gomez, here to see Lieutenant Mahoney and Captain Webber," he muttered under his breath before giving me back my driver's license. "Er... Gomez. Twice. That's interesting."

I held back a sigh. A little stalling would do me no harm and him a little good. "My family is from Puerto Rico, and we're given our father's surname, followed by our mother's surname there. My parents happened to have the same surname. But they weren't cousins." If I had a dime for every time I'd been asked if they were cousins, I could've hired a top private detective long ago and bypassed the sheriff's department altogether. The department had a decent enough reputation, and a few here had been kind to me, but my parents' case wasn't among their successes.

"Why not, um, just use one Gomez and save time?" he asked with a subtle glance at the door behind him.

"Because my mother's side, who all still live in Puerto Rico, would be deeply offended if I didn't use their Gomez, too. I tried telling them that I could simply use the one and make it *their* Gomez and that the other side would never know, but the idea of the other side thinking I was using only *their* Gomez was even more offensive." I gave him a moment to unpack that. My family dynamics could be as hard to explain as they were to understand.

I like to think of my family's two sides as the Practical Gomezes and the Magical Gomezes. The practical side is my mom's side, and they are all about following tradition, unless and until tradition becomes too expensive to follow. My mother grew up eating rice, beans, roots, and a piece of meat every single day for dinner and as next-day leftovers for lunch, going to church every Sunday, and studying diligently so she could get into a good college and follow a career path that would guarantee life-long security. Which she did. Until she met my dad. Then she became practical-*ish*.

The magical side is my dad's side. They insist that supernatural abilities run strong in our blood and that we must use these abilities for the greater good. We have *curanderos (*healers*), brujas and brujos (*witches, all good*), santeros (*santería practitioners, most of them good; one evil*), espiritistas (*spiritits), and the random strange ability here and there. Do I believe it? Let's just say that I fully believe that they believe it.

Magical Gomezes still live on the island, but most are spread among seven states, four countries, and three continents. My dad, who was born and raised in the Bronx, spent his summers running wild along the northwest beaches of Puerto Rico and humoring his grandmother by carving out Ouija boards from shipwrecks. He was encouraged to follow what he thought of as "instincts", and they thought of as "psychic gifts" in finding lost treasures, without a care for his safety or the future. Which he did. Until he met my mom. Then he became magical-*ish*.

I smiled at Corporal Rover good-naturedly, after giving him a minute, and signaled to the door behind him to remind him why I was here. He cleared his throat, and the way he looked at me, thoughtful yet determined, made it clear that he was about to get rid of me as nicely as possible. Before he could open his mouth to deny me, I took a deep breath and reluctantly took a different tack. "Look, I'm here because my parents were murdered twelve years ago, and not only has your department never solved the case, but they never tell me anything at all, no matter how many times I come here and *beg*. But Lieutenant Mahoney is new, and I have hope that maybe I can get through to him. That's why I'm here. Let me in to see him, *please*."

Corporal Rover froze.

I ran a hand through my hair, trying not to let exasperation mount. I got that the corporal was new, and he didn't want to get into trouble, but what was wrong with people? Was real compassion dead? Because I was tired of the fake kind from people like Captain Webber, that only got you a pat on the head and no answers. "Just tell them that I blackmailed you into announcing me right now, without an appointment," I said to him. "Tell them I said I'd go straight to the news again to call Lieutenant Mahoney out before he's even begun. Reporters are only interested in my parents every three years or so when there's a lag in sensational stories, but maybe news about how the new supervisor won't even talk to a double murder victims' daughter will grab their attention."

He snapped out of it. "No! I don't need to tell them that. You're right. He *owes* it to you to see you, and I'll be happy to tell him that. I—I'm sorry for your loss."

I tried to smile, and I gave him a nod because now, no matter what happened with the lieutenant, I had a little bit of faith again. Now I really didn't want Rover to get in trouble. "Tell him that I have new information on the case, too," I half-lied. The Corporal turned and knocked on the door he'd been guarding, and a deep voice on the other side told him to come in. A sharp sort of shiver ran half-way down my spine, like lightning, at the sound of that voice. The Magical Gomezes would call it a premonition. I called it hope.

Moments later, Rover, trying hard to look encouraging but looking more like a puppy who'd been scolded, motioned me in. When I turned to face the room, the first person I saw was Captain Webber, who I'd never liked. He took one look at my smile and gave Rover a nearly imperceptible eye-roll. Did he think I had flirted my way into his office?

"Thank you, Corporal Rover," I managed. "I know you were intent on following orders, but I was certain those orders didn't include ignoring both a victims' daughter for the twelfth straight year *and* vital information on their very cold case."

Rover gave everyone an uncertain look as he hovered by the door. Captain Webber heaved himself from his chair, and I stuck my hand out to greet him. "I blackmailed Corporal Rover into announcing me," I explained, hoping it would let the Corporal off the hook.

Webber raised an eyebrow and showed me his teeth (his attempt at a smile). In all the years I'd known him, I had never seen the corners of his eyes crease. "You're confessing to a serious crime, Angie." The last time I'd seen him, he'd squeezed my shoulder while ordering me to let the adults handle everything. I hadn't been allowed in to see him since.

Instead, he always sent the message that the department was on the case. "But I'll let it slide since it seems you've got friends in high places nowadays." I gave him a curious look, and he explained. "You did a great job with the mayor's bust."

I couldn't tell if he was joking or being patronizing with the 'friends in high places' bit. Everyone knew Mayor Sandberg. She was one of the subjects I'd sculpted that I liked as a person. I focused on the tip of his hawkish nose and tried to look appreciative.

"Thank you. The mayor has such beautiful bone structure that she was a pleasure to sculpt." It was through Mayor Sandberg that I learned Webber was about to be promoted again. He had once sat behind the very desk Brian Mahoney was leaning against now. I knew it was the same desk because I had carved my initials into the side of it once when he wasn't looking, so he wouldn't forget a thirteen-year-old girl was waiting for answers. It had been an impulsive move. My glance skipped past Lieutenant Mahoney to see if they were still there.

They were—right under the spot where Mahoney was resting his fingers.

My attention was brought back to Rover when he asked, "Are you a plastic surgeon?" It took me a moment to understand. "Oh. Um, no. *Bust* as in *statue.* I'm a sculptor." Rover turned pink yet again, and Captain Webber ushered him out of the door and took his leave.

When the door closed shut, I turned to face Lieutenant Mahoney. Our eyes met and held. A curious sensation rushed through me. It was as if everything inside me lurched forward, then fluttered around without knowing where to settle again.

And I felt like *something* in me was being mirrored in *something* in him. Which was a decidedly magical Gomez thought. The second of the day. One a week was the norm. Abuela Luci would be ecstatic.

Right now, though, she'd say, "*Mueve la colita*," which literally meant shake your tail and figuratively meant either shake your booty or get going, depending on the context. And that's what I did. Get going, that is. Not shake my booty. I stuck out my hand and introduced myself. Only the handshake lasted a smidgeon too long, and there was no reason for our eyes to lock again, but they did.

Maybe he recognized me? Brian Mahoney had been three years ahead of me in Chaminade-Julienne, a local Catholic High School, and his older brother, Sean, had been one year ahead of him, and his younger brother, Patrick, one year behind.

We dropped each other's hands. "Angie Gomez Gomez," he repeated, before asking, "Was this you?" He motioned to the side of the desk where his fingers swept across the "AGG" I had carved.

Again, my spine shivered. I straightened to stop it. "Yes. I carved it with a sharp pen once when Captain Webber was called to the door. I wanted him to remember that a thirteen-year-old girl was waiting for answers."

He nodded. "Corporal Rover explained why you're here. I know everyone must always say the same thing, but I'm deeply sorry for your loss. I can't imagine what it was like. I'm also sorry we haven't solved the case. I'm glad you came to see me." To his credit, he seemed sincere. Our eyes met once more, but thank the stars, whimsy was gone, and I was feeling practical again.

"Thank you," I said. It had taken me years to be able to discuss my parents' murders without becoming emotional. Time had allowed me to develop coping mechanisms and to accept that the dull, throbbing ache behind my heart would always be there, even when my heart continued to beat and allow me to live. It was only when the sheriff's department ignored me (and sometimes at night, and often during happy events) that grief and frustrations came back and struck me hard. Right now, I was holding on to the little bit of faith that Corporal Rover had gifted me.

The lieutenant leaned back against his desk and motioned for me to sit. "I remember when your family first moved here," he continued. "It was exciting that a renowned treasure hunter would be moving here, of all places."

That surprised me. Though it had made local news when my parents came here, nothing stayed an event anymore. Information overload made the world move on too quickly for that. I gave him a cautious nod and looked out the window, where the fall sky was more gray than blue. 'Of all places' was right. Too many things had never made sense to me…

"And Corporal Rover mentioned you have new, vital information?" he asked, bringing me back.

I turned from the window and took a moment to study him the way I'd studied Corporal Rover. Wavy, obsidian hair, Atlantic blue eyes, set deep, a near replica of Michael Angelo's *David's* nose, and thin lips that quirked in a good-humored sort of way. Despite this, his expression gave nothing away. "Have you looked over the file?" I asked, doubting it.

The Mahoney's were well known and regarded in the region. His older brother was now District Attorney, his dad was a respected state representative, and his mom was one of four hosts on the daily noon show, *Life in Dayton*. Each took their standing in the community seriously. His younger brother was in med school, and I'd heard his mom somehow managed to mention this fact on air at least once a month. Brian Mahoney had moved away after high school and had been away for years, so it remained to be seen how serious he was, either about his position, his standing in the community, or both.

"Yes. I did. You stated your father always wore an amber pendant around his neck, and it was the only missing item. You believe the perpetrator was after the pendant."

I nodded. "My mom's purse and my dad's wallet were still on them, and a dog got away from its owner and was heard barking before the..." I stopped and took a deep breath before rushing on. "Before the shots were fired. The dog was still with my parents when they were found. This evidence led detectives to believe that the dog interrupted the burglary, and it all went wrong. But I believe the perpetrator got what he or she wanted—my dad's amber pendant. Only no one took my theory about why they were after the pendant seriously. Did you?"

"I did."

"And?"

He gave me a cautious look. "No one except you ever saw or heard of this pendant."

I sighed. "And why isn't my word enough? Why would I make that up? I'm telling you what was stolen. It's called a *lead*."

He studied me for a moment, and I got the feeling he was choosing his next words carefully. "I don't believe that you're making the amber pendant up, Miss Gomez, but you're claiming this pendant was the motive for the crime. For it to be a motive, it would need to be important to somebody." His voice and gaze were gentle. Mine were hard.

"I told them why it was important."

He nodded. "Let's try again. I know this is hard to talk about, and I know we have your long-ago statement, but why don't you walk me through your theory one more time?"

"So I feel listened to? No, thanks. I'm done with being patronized." I stood up. It was all so frustrating and maddening! I had no power. No connections. Throughout the years, I had even hired a few private detectives. They had charged me exorbitant fees and come up with nothing. I couldn't keep doing that, not if I wanted to take care of my grandmother when she reached old age.

"No. Because I want to hear everything directly from you. Reading someone's words is not the same as listening to them." He folded his arms across his chest, calmly, as if I hadn't just accused him of being patronizing. "Start at the beginning. How did a treasure hunter from Puerto Rico end up in Ohio?"

I raised an eyebrow. "You want me to start there?"

"Yes."

"Why?"

"Because in everyone's past, there's a crazy string of coincidences that brought them to where they are. For example, I'm in Dayton partly because a great grandmother wanted to avoid marrying an unattractive neighbor who had followed her from Limerick in Ireland to New York. So, she bought a train ticket to the furthest place she could afford. Dayton." It was the kind of comment that my dad would have loved, and it made me smile even as it made my heart hurt to imagine the silly, philosophical ramblings he would have gone off on. He smiled back. "I think if you tell me the crazy string that brought your parents here, I might be able to see the case through your eyes."

"Well, it's definitely crazy." After a moment's hesitation, I sat back down, took a small breath, and began to talk. "My dad was an anthropologist with knowledge of the Taíno language, spoken by the indigenous people of Puerto Rico. He also had an amazing ability to read between the lines of historical documents and then make connections between everything he'd read. It's complicated, but it all led to the discovery of the location of *San Tomás*, a ship that sunk in the Bermuda Triangle in 1596. *San Tomás* was known to be carrying loads of gold, but my father believed it was also carrying what the Spaniards thought was the key to the Fountain of Youth."

I looked up then, and he seemed riveted. Everyone loved a good story. But this one ended in disappointment. I licked my lips and continued. "But locating and exploring shipwrecks takes money. Lots of it. My dad had a good reputation, and he received several offers from deep-sea exploration companies. He chose Tesorex because their goals aligned with his own. And this is where my mom comes in," I added. "She was a sonar and radar systems engineer with Tesorex, and she played a huge role in finding *San Tomás*. They fell in love at sea, the captain of the sea vessel they were on married them, and I was born in the middle of the Bermuda triangle, four weeks ahead of schedule and a few months before they located the shipwreck."

"You were born in the middle of the Bermuda triangle?" he repeated, looking nonplussed.

"Yes," I said with a smile because I liked that detail about my life. It connected me to my parents' adventurous past. "Long story short, they found nineteen metric tons of gold and some amber, but there was a huge lawsuit about who owned the gold. Tesorex meant for it to go to the people of various Caribbean islands and Mexico because it had been stolen from them. To my parents' huge disappointment, the Spanish government won, and it was all sent to Spain. Tesorex was left with only the amber, even though they had invested huge amounts of money. They almost went belly-up, but they were bought by Sonrad Technologies, based here in Dayton, due to the advances they had made with adaptive radar, sonar, and signal processing," I explained, and he nodded.

Sonrad was a well-known contractor for Wright Patterson, the largest air force base in the country. "My mom took a job with them, and the University of Dayton offered my dad a position as a professor and researcher. After the roller-coaster ride they'd been on, my parents felt that Dayton offered a nice change of pace. It also has a rich history, and they liked that."

Lieutenant Mahoney looked away and became pensive. After a while, he asked, "And the amber pendant you speak of was made from amber found in the *San Tomás*?"

I nodded. "Yes. It was unique. Round with black spots, reminiscent of the sun. He said the dark spots in the amber they'd found were gnat pupa, but…" I hesitated.

"But?" he leaned forward.

I took a deep breath and let it out. "You know what I'm going to say. Tesorex supposedly lost track of the amber, but I don't think they did. And while the official story was that my parents worked for the University of Dayton and Sonrad, they used to drive off to work together all the time. To the air force base. I think they were working on something else. I believe the gnat pupa was special." I swallowed, knowing how ridiculous it sounded. I wasn't embarrassed, but I needed to be taken seriously for once. Even though I knew the lieutenant had already read my long-ago statement, there was no way to talk about gnat pupa, the fountain of youth, and government coverups without sounding nutty. Also, I was thirteen when I gave that statement. I was now twenty-five.

When I mentioned on-air once that I believed my parents' murders were related to their work with the Air Force, the Department of Defense called it a conspiracy theory. My parents' murders had been a burglary gone wrong according to the powers that be. But I was sure it was more than that. A few people online rallied behind me. Unfortunately, they were people who blogged about Sasquatch, the Loch Ness Monster, leprechauns, and pixies.

"University of Dayton and Sonrad are the two main local contractors for the base," Lieutenant Mahoney pointed out. "A lot of their employees work at Wright Patterson."

"Yes, and it makes sense for my mom to have worked on-site there. She was an engineer. But my dad was an anthropologist. Why would *he* be at the base? And only my mom knew he wore that amber pendant. He kept it hidden, even from me, but I was nosy and observant. I think he knew he had to protect at least one of the amber stones that looked like the sun because it held information. And I'm certain he knew what the information was. Despite his reputation for taking risks, my dad was also responsible. If the information the stones held was powerful, he would've reported it to the United States Government. I believe that's the real reason we ended up here. But something must have gone wrong." I leaned forward. "There's a saying in Spanish, that a secret between two people is no longer a secret. I think whatever they were working on was leaked to the wrong people…" My voice trailed off again because his face had gone blank.

After a long silence, he finally said, "Thank you. I promise I'll take it all into consideration."

"What does that even mean?" I asked, not bothering to hide my frustration.

"It means I'm taking you seriously. I know our department failed to keep victims' families in the loop in the past and caused further pain. I intend to change that. Cold case files still under our jurisdiction are a priority for me." He hesitated a moment before looking me in the eye. "Do you remember being asked if your mother was wearing valuable jewelry that day?"

"Yes. Both my grandmother and I were asked. We both answered that she wasn't because she didn't own anything other than run-of-the-mill diamond studs. She didn't like wearing jewelry."

He nodded, and his lips tightened as if he were about to say something unpleasant. I braced myself. "In the days leading up to the crime, your mother was overheard describing a necklace your dad had commissioned for her out of metals and stones he recovered from the first wreck he salvaged and saying that she would be wearing it the night of the reception. Detectives believe this information could have spread, and it could have led to them being held up. I'm sorry you were never told."

That threw me, and my mind reeled as it tried to latch on to the only piece of information I had ever been given. *My mom was overheard describing a necklace my dad commissioned for her and saying that she would be wearing it the night of the reception?* Slowly, I shook my head. "Whoever said that lied. My dad never commissioned a necklace for my mom. He made one for her. It was heavy and clunky and had fallen apart a few times. It was a joke between them, and my mom treasured it because my dad made it, not because it had any market value. She wouldn't have told anyone that she'd ever wear it because it was in pieces."

He carefully countered with, "But can you see how someone hearing bits and pieces of her story about the necklace could have misconstrued it? It could also account for your dad's pendant being stolen instead. Our detectives sent your description of it to a nationwide database that pawnshops and dealers use, but there's never been a match."

My chest began to hurt. Value was mistakenly attached to one necklace, and then the wrong necklace was stolen instead. It was possible. Why wasn't I told before? And why had

Lieutenant Mahoney encouraged me to go on and on about my theory if he believed he already had the answer?

I turned to look out the window without seeing while I sifted through muddled thoughts, feelings, and information. Someone at some point must have lied about what my mom said that night. My mom always laughed when she spoke of the necklace. The way she described it would never have led others to believe it was valuable, and she would never have said that she was wearing it to a fancy event. Well, maybe to make my dad laugh.

I felt a headache coming on, and I rubbed my head. "Who said my mom had been talking about this necklace?" I finally asked. He looked at me steadily but didn't say a word. I folded my arms over my chest. "You said you would be more forthcoming."

"I did, and we will be. You have the right to be kept up to date about the investigation's status, but we can't divulge anything that compromises it. Unfortunately, divulging the witness's name, in this case, would discourage others from coming forward, and people do decide to come forward years later, Miss Gomez. Fear sometimes holds them back until guilt becomes more powerful. But speaking of new information, you said you had something new and vital to share."

Oh, he was good. He'd kindly listened before dropping a bomb that raised doubts in me about my long-held theory. Now he was carefully dismissing me, likely thinking that he'd saved himself from ever having to listen to my theories ever again.

I sprang up, suddenly in a better mood now that I could dismiss the sheriff's office now and forever. "Here's my new information, Lieutenant." Interest sparked in his eyes. "You're going to sorely regret not having more foresight today." I had all my mom's old planners. I planned to study them to find out where she had been in the days leading up to the crime. From there, I'd begin my own investigation. It was a start. I finally had something. And because a part of me felt grateful to Brian Mahoney for giving me that something, I gave him a half-smile and a salute. I then turned and walked to the door.

He reached it a split-second after me and put his hand on the knob, presumably to open it for me. When he didn't, I looked up to catch him studying me. "Your father's mother is Señora Lucinda, the owner of *Tea and Spirits* in the Oregon District?" He phrased it as a question, though it was clear he knew the answer.

Tea and Spirits was popular for miles around. The spirits part did not refer to liquor. It referred to how my Abuela Luci, and countless others, believed she could read a person's aura and fortune. The tea part was good ole healing teas she imported from Puerto Rico. I shot him a warning glance. I never took kindly to anyone mocking her purported abilities. "Yes. Why?"

"I'm trying to determine if your words about my regrets are a psychic vision or a threat," he said, also trying to end things on a friendly note.

I crossed my heart and said, "They're an entirely legal vow." Yes, he had given me something, but he was also part of the system that had withheld information from me for too long.

as Anthony Pappalardo of River's Bend Funeral Home, agreed with an impatient nod.

"But the mayor is *dead*," I reminded them.

"I recall," Anthony replied. "She's at the morgue, and half of her face is missing. You recently sculpted her. You're an artist. You know her face well. You're the best person for the job."

I heard Abuela Luci's sharp intake of breath, and I turned to give her an incredulous look. I knew exactly what she was thinking: a change in professional circumstances, the cards had foretold it. But working on dead people's faces? After five years at the University of Cincinnati's prestigious DAAP School of Design? No.

I turned next to Mr. Pappalardo and gave him the same look. Mother Nature must have taken away from him in brains what she had given to him in muscles. "Sculpting the mayor using clay and reconstructing *her face* are two very different things."

"I read your bio. You also volunteer as a makeup artist with Gem City Theatre Group, which means you have a cosmetology license. You'll need one," he said as if I hadn't said a word. "The state of Ohio requires the license for postmortem work, and it's perfect that you will be able to do the mayor's makeup, too."

Abuela Luci squeezed my shoulder and said, "You should do it."

My eyebrows rose to my hairline as I turned to stare at her. "No!"

"Why not? It's not like you don't need the money."

"It's a *dead body*."

"It will be a *fully embalmed* dead body," the man said. "Stiff. No blood. Like working on marble, maybe." He shrugged.

Words deserted me.

"Pull her heartstrings," Abuela instructed him. "The turquoise glows brightly in her aura. It does in yours, too."

Anthony Pappalardo studied Abuela. He must've read something in her expression because he nodded and fixed his surprisingly soulful, hazel eyes on me. "It's my granddad's business. He used to be one of the most talented postmortem reconstruction specialists in the nation, but his arthritis has been bad for years, and he's had trouble finding his equal. He's lost a lot of business. Now that I'm back home, I can see how bad it's gotten. I'm trying to help, but I'm no artist. The last cosmetologist we hired died last night. The mayor chose us for her prepaid funeral plan about a year ago when she was promoting local businesses. This is a huge opportunity for us, Miss Gomez Gomez. Holding her memorial and funeral service is a once in a lifetime chance for us, but we need to do it right. Would you at least take a look at her?" He gestured toward the door. "Pappa, my granddad, is waiting at the morgue."

"Who thought of asking me. You, or your grandfather?" That would be the deciding factor. If it were the grandfather, I'd say yes to at least taking a look. Even though it was crazy.

"Brenda Mumford."

My eyebrows shot up again. "Mayor Sandberg's daughter?" I had only met her once, when I sketched the mayor before beginning work on her bust. I had gently pointed out to the mayor that I preferred to sculpt her mouth the way I saw it in her face, to make the bust more life-like, rather than from an old photograph she had given me. Brenda had approved.

Anthony nodded. "When I explained our predicament, she remembered how impressed her mom was with your work. And my grandfather allowed himself to hope."

Moments later, I was staring at Anthony's motorcycle and considering my sarong skirt. I had taken the trolley to Abuela's shop. The morgue was a twenty-minute walk away. If I didn't want to keep Anthony's grandfather waiting, I would have to show some leg. "Don't worry, sweetie," Abuela Luci called from the door. "He's not interested in your legs." I cast a glance heavenward before taking the helmet Anthony handed me.

"Is your grandmother always this loud?"

"Yes."

"And does she always wave her hands around in the air like that?"

"She's not waving her hands around in the air," I answered, waving my hands around in the air until I caught myself. "She's gesturing. It's called being expressive." The motorcycle came to life then, and we were off.

As we roared and stopped, repeatedly, down the wide city streets designed for a once populous and popular city, I mentally reviewed what I knew about Mayor Sandberg's case.

Shot to death in her home office. No security cameras surrounded her home. There was gossip that it all had to do with an old building and a controversial vote.

In 1917, the Wright Brothers made Dayton, already a gem in Ohio's industrialization era, the birthplace of flight. Now, after years of manufacturing job losses and urban exodus, it was enjoying a renaissance of sorts. But lifelong residents were slowly being priced out. The owner of Woodruff Place, an ornate tower built in 1910 that sat two blocks away from where the Wright Brothers and famous poet Paul Lawrence Dunbar had grown up together, had gone bankrupt. The city bought it for a song. Half the city commission wanted to condemn and raze the Woodruff and build a high-end mixed-use tower in its place. The other half wanted to rehabilitate it and turn the apartments into below-market-rate condominiums. Mayor Sandberg had cast the decisive vote for rehabilitation. Residents applauded her; businesses did not. Armchair detectives speculated that some greedy soul was looking for the possibility of a new vote with a new mayor.

Montgomery County's Coroner's office came into view, and I felt my gut tighten. What the hell was I doing?

We parked next to a vintage, powder blue hearse, and I struggled to climb off the motorcycle without flashing the security guard out front. When I caught my reflection on the door leading to the morgue, a combination of helmet hair and long, frizzy brown waves greeted me. Anthony handed me a wide-tooth comb from his back pocket. Maybe he wasn't so bad.

Brenda Mumford and Anthony Pappalardo's grandfather, a hunched, limping older man with kind eyes who introduced himself as Pappa, were waiting in the lobby. Brenda's eyes were red and swollen, and my heart squeezed. After exchanging subdued introductions and greetings, Brenda grabbed my hand and said. "I thought of you because we were all so impressed with your work, and my mom…" she paused to take a breath "…the lower left part of her face..."

I studied Brenda's attractive face, realizing how much she looked like her mother, while I tried to guess the extent of the damage to the mayor.

"I'll explain everything to Miss Gomez, don't you worry," Pappa said to her in a soothing tone. "If you'd like, you can wait for us in the room over there. They have both coffee and tea."

Brenda wiped at her eyes with a tissue and nodded in agreement. When she was safely inside the room, Pappa turned his concerned gaze on me, and I saw the telltale signs of glaucoma. "Tilly Sandberg needs extensive work done on the lower left quadrant of her face and some on the right side of her skull. I used to be an artist, but I can no longer handle anything but skull-work. I tried to hire the tri-state area's best postmortem cosmetic reconstruction specialist, but he's not available." He paused to look at me with his kind, watery eyes as if to gauge how I was taking it. I still didn't how I was feeling about it all, but I offered him a smile, and he continued. "When Brenda suggested you, she explained how important it was to her that her mother's mouth looks exactly the way it does on the bust you sculpted of her, and she thought you might be able to transfer your skills. If you cannot, which would be understandable, she will need to take her mother to Welcome Home Funeral Parlors," he explained, mentioning the largest funeral home in the Dayton area.

I nodded, careful not to show Pappa that I understood far more than he was letting on. The stakes were now higher. His business, River's Bend Funeral Home, was in decline. And now their cosmetologist was dead. I liked Pappa. All my instincts told me he was a good man fallen on hard times. I pushed my concerns away for the moment and said, "Let's take a look at Tilly Sandberg."

The three of us walked down a hallway until Pappa stopped in front of the Administrator's Office. A female voice on the other side laughed and said, "Right. I'll see you next Friday night at eight."

Pappa turned a sad smile our way. "We're surrounded by death, but people are still making plans for a Friday night. I like these little reminders that life goes on for the living."

The door opened then, and Lieutenant Brian Mahoney filled the frame. He was wearing a dark suit, white shirt, and striped tie, like last time, and I was close enough to smell his aftershave. My insides twisted in a way I didn't like, and I took two steps back.

His startled gaze took me in before bouncing to Pappa, who greeted him in the familiar way of old friends before introducing his grandson and then me.

"Miss Gomez Gomez and I have already met," Lieutenant Mahoney said as he shook our hands in turn.

"You can call me Angie," I said with a forced smile.

"Angie," he repeated. "What brings you to the coroner's office?" I nearly smiled at that. He was suspicious of me now because of the vow I'd made to him. It made me feel like I had the upper hand somehow. The upper hand of what, though, I didn't know.

"She's with me," Pappa said by way of explanation, and I nodded. "That's right. I'm with him."

Lieutenant Mahoney fixed his eyes on me, and I raised my right eyebrow. If he thought I was going to expand on that explanation, he was mistaken. The door opened wide then, and a pretty redhead poked her head out. "Is everything alright, Brian?" she asked, putting a hand on Mahoney's arm as she looked past him.

"Yes. Just catching up with Pappa here. I'm sure you know him."

The redhead smiled. "Of course. He picks up bodies a few times a month."

A few times a month? I hid my dismay. Business must really be bad for Pappa if he was only picking up at the county morgue a few times a month. Unless the natural-cause, no-autopsy-needed type of death business was booming.

"He brought a team along with him today," Brian continued, clearly still fishing for my reason for being there.

I quickly introduced both myself and Anthony before Pappa could tell her why we were there.

"Oh, you're the one Brenda Mumford was telling me about," the redhead said. "I'm Joanna Danes, the administrative coordinator. Is Mrs. Mumford here, too?"

"She's in the waiting room," Pappa explained.

"Come this way, then. I don't want to keep the poor thing waiting any longer than she has to." Joanna said goodbye to Mahoney, who replied with, "See you next Friday," before moving aside to hold the door open for us. I brought up the rear, and when I passed him, said, "I wonder where we'll bump into each other next, Lieutenant!"

The corner of his mouth lifted. "I can't think of many places where we're both needed in a professional capacity. I'm guessing you're here because you recently sculpted Mayor Sandberg's bust, and Mrs. Mumford wanted you to advise on reconstruction."

I smiled. "Good guess about why I'm here. You're close to the truth but not quite there. I, however, was way off the mark about why you're here. I *never* would've guessed that it was in a *professional* capacity." I glanced at Joanna, who was halfway across the room, because he'd clearly been making a date with her.

"You're close to the truth, but not quite there." He shrugged one shoulder, smiled, and walked away.

"I'll leave you here, Pappa, since you're authorized, but I'll be at my desk if you need me," Joanna said as she closed the door to the room we had just entered.

Fluorescent lights were shining down on metal tables covered with sheets. When my eyes adjusted to the bright light, I saw the metal tables had feet sticking out of them. There were bodies beneath those blankets. I shut my eyes and swallowed hard. Did I want to do this?

Anthony reached us, and both he and Pappa began clamoring for answers. "What's wrong?!" and "What happened?!" they asked.

"What do you mean, *what's wrong*? Didn't you hear her?" I shouted back.

"Hear who?" Anthony asked.

"Mayor Sandberg!"

Two pairs of eyes in two dismayed faces looked at me like I had windmills in my head.

The door opened, and another "What's wrong!" came from it. I turned. It was Joanna.

I would *not* have her telling Brian Mahoney that I was crazy. The very thought made me gather myself enough to say, "I stepped back and almost fell on…" I read the tag on the cot behind me. "…Mr. Kazinsky, and I screamed. That's all. I'm so sorry I startled you." I swallowed hard to keep down the panic that was rising. Hopefully, she'd buy it and leave. I wasn't sure how much longer I could keep it together.

"Yes." Pappa's head bobbed up and down. "She tripped, but we caught her just in time."

"But, I heard two screams."

"The second was, er, mine. I didn't want my friend here joining a dead man on a cot," Anthony quickly explained, and I was grateful. He barely knew me, but his instinct was to help me.

"Oh." Joanna shrugged. "I guess I can see how almost falling onto a corpse could be scary. Don't worry about it. No one else heard. Are you almost done here?" she asked.

"We're still consulting," Pappa replied.

"All right. I'll leave you to it." She took one last look at me and left.

The moment the door closed shut, I turned to them, "You heard her the second time, right?"

"Joanna Danes?" Anthony asked.

"No! Mayor Sandberg!"

Anthony's eyes were wide as his eyes flitted from me to his grandfather and then me again. "Er, no. I didn't." He turned to his grandfather, asking, "Did, uh, you?" in a voice meant to appease me.

Pappa cleared his throat. "What exactly did you hear, dear?"

"I'm not seeing windmills *or* giants," I insisted, using an old defense of my dad's.

"Giants," Pappa repeated before lifting his hand to feel my forehead, no longer bothering to hide his concern for my mental wellbeing.

"From *Don Quixote*," Anthony explained to him. "She means she's not mistaking windmills for giants."

"Yes." Somewhere within my confusion, it made me happy that Anthony understood the reference. My mom used to enjoy quoting from Don Quixote and thinking about the story, quotes, and characters in times of trouble had become a

Anthony guided me down the row of cots toward Doug, the cosmetologist. When we were beside him, he gestured grandly with his hands, subtly glancing at his watch as he did so. I knew then that he was only humoring his granddad.

I took a deep breath, held it in, lowered my head cot-level, and began to gingerly move from Doug's feet to his head, with my head as close to the body as I was comfortable with. When I got to the head, I heard a voice croak, "Kathy, Kathy! Call 911. My arm!"

I gasped. I hadn't expected anything to happen! I was hoping for some other explanation. "Who's Kathy?"

Pappa's face went pale. "His wife."

"Did he mention his arm? Did he die of a heart attack?" I asked in an increasingly panicked tone that mimicked what I'd heard. Pappa nodded, Anthony went as still as a statue, and I felt as if the blood had drained from my body. My heart began beating so fast I was afraid I'd need a cot of my own.

I was a Magical Gomez.

THREE

> *"Wayfarer, there is no path; the path is made as you walk.*
>
> ANTONIO MACHADO, POET FROM SPAIN

Panicked thoughts rushed at me. *Have I always had this ability? Would I have realized it earlier if I had gotten closer to my mom and dad at their wakes? Would I have learned the name of their murderer?*

That last thought had me seeking a chair. Anthony noticed and guided me to a stool.

All these years I hadn't believed my grandmother—or anyone in the family—when they insisted they had magical gifts. My parents' explanations about instincts and natural inclinations made more sense. Until now. I had just heard two dead people's last words. That was neither instinct nor inclination. It was magic or paranormal ability. Nothing else explained it.

"All this time, I might have had the one gift that could have told me who killed my parents," I whispered, barely able to breathe. Someone squeezed my shoulder and I looked up to see Pappa's kind eyes looking into mine. "I stayed by the door during my parents' wake," I said to him. "They looked cold... and grey. Not like themselves. I didn't want to remember them that way. But if I had gotten closer, I might have heard their last words. I might have learned who killed them." I shook my head, realizing he might not know what I was talking about. "My parents, they were—"

"We know about your parents," he said gently. "But you can't do this to yourself. It's completely normal to avoid deceased loved ones who don't look like themselves. It's why I take my job so seriously. You didn't know what you didn't know. Focus on the here and now."

Anthony kneeled in front of me. "Yes. Think about it, Angie. We have a victim, and now we have a name. Bonnie."

I gazed at him unseeingly as I let it all sink in. "You believe me?" I finally asked.

Anthony looked away for a moment and shook his head. "Truth is, I don't know what to believe. But I'm intrigued enough to look into Mayor Sandberg's life and see if she knew anyone named Bonnie."

Slowly, I nodded. Focus on the here and now, Pappa said. We had a name. "Yes. Let's do that."

The sound of voices reached me (live ones this time), and I looked at Pappa and Anthony. Other bodies needed to be identified and picked up. We wouldn't be alone much longer. "Promise me that what happened here won't leave this room," I begged.

Anthony let out a harsh laugh. "Of course not. Who would believe us?"

Pappa frowned in concern. "No one would believe us, but some would ask you to prove it, and if you did, your life as you know it would be over."

"Half the world's law enforcement would be after you. Wright Patterson Air Force Base would probably reach you first since they're around the corner," Anthony added.

Pappa nodded sagely. "They'd lock you up with the aliens in hangar eighteen to study you."

I didn't know whether to laugh or shudder. Hangar eighteen, where the Roswell aliens were rumored to have been stored, was the stuff of legends.

The voices outside grew closer, and I stood up. "Let's go. I'm not up for small talk."

Pappa took over. "You two load the mayor onto the hearse. I'll get back to Brenda Mumford. We've already left her waiting too long." He turned to me. "I can't begin to imagine how you're feeling, and I hate to pressure you, but will you work on the mayor?"

I managed a smile, thankful that he was giving me something practical to hold onto. "Yes. I'll work on Mayor Sandberg, and I'm confident I'll do a good job."

River's Bend Funeral Home was soon before us. Georgian brick, white columns, black shutters, four bay windows, and round shrubbery interspersed with flowers lining the path. Two stories in the front, three in the back. It was simple and pleasant to behold. A long, paved driveway led down to additional parking in the back. The cemetery beyond was dotted with white and gray stones, gorgeous oaks, and beyond that, the river. The parts together made a peaceful whole, but on closer inspection, I could see missing mortar, loose bricks, and weeds growing between cracks in the sidewalks.

The funeral home hugged one side of a horseshoe tucked into Dayton's Miami River. The neighborhood I had moved into about six months ago (when Abuela had gently told me my early hours were cramping her style), McPherson Town, hugged the other side, about a ten-minute walk away.

Pappa drove down the long driveway and parked in reverse. Anthony was already there, and we helped him unload the cot, roll it up a ramp, and into the embalming room on the lower level. It was strange how it didn't feel strange.

I had expected the astringent smell, fluorescent lights, and cold temperature. But I had also been expecting glaring, stark white walls, and metal cabinets and countertops, like at the county morgue. Instead, sky blue walls with an assortment of black and white prints of New York City decorated the room. White cabinets with stainless steel countertops and white tile backsplash lined the perimeter of the room. A bright light shone on three metal tables with something that looked like a toilet and drain at the end of each. I guessed it was an embalming machine. A small rolling table and adjustable stool were next to the middle table.

A loud sliding sound caught my attention and I looked over to see Anthony had opened one of six drawers in a large stainless steel fridge on the far wall near the back door. He folded back a white blanket to reveal a deceased older woman. "Do it again," he said to me, gesturing to the woman's head.

"Anthony, that's enough!" Pappa scolded him. "This is bordering on irreverence."

I sent Pappa a hopeful glance. "I'd like to do it one more time. Now that we're here, there's a part of me that's wondering if I imagined it all."

"Me too," Anthony admitted. "On the way over I was thinking how you might have been spooked by all the dead bodies. It could have caused you to hallucinate."

"Then how do you explain her knowing Doug's last words?" Pappa asked.

"We don't know if those were Doug's last words. All we know is he died of a heart attack, which is not uncommon," Anthony pointed out.

"She heard him say Kathy's name," Pappa countered. "How on earth did she guess his wife's name?"

"Kathy is a fairly common name."

Pappa gave him a look.

"Please let me listen one more time?" I pled. "For my own peace of mind."

"Why don't you listen to the mayor again, instead?"

Anthony shook his head. "She should listen to Mrs. Perez because I know what her last words were. Her niece told me."

Pappa's eyes widened. "Why didn't you say so? That changes everything. It'll be a scientific experiment in search of proof positive and not an intrusion." He gestured grandly toward Mrs. Perez and I walked over.

Slowly, I lowered my head toward hers. When I was two inches away, I heard her gravelly voice say, "Your breath smells." This time, instead of shock, I felt a deep thrill. This was real!

"Well?" Anthony asked.

"Your breath smells," I repeated.

Anthony's lips twitched and he nodded once. "Those were her last words to her son. The whole family heard, and they laughed over it."

The three of us looked at each other, and I could tell they were feeling the same excitement I was.

"Bonnie is dead," Anthony repeated, rushing over to the mayor. Pappa and I followed. "We know a murdered person's last words, but we can't take the information to the police because we have no way of explaining how we know." He looked up, his eyes sparkling. "Which means we have to investigate ourselves until we have something we can take to them." He looked over the body with a critical eye. "Impossible to know for sure without forensics, but from what I've seen, I think the damage indicates the murderer was in front of Mayor Sandberg when they shot her, but at a distance." He motioned the action.

Pappa examined her fingernails, hands, wrists, neck, and face as I watched. "And she doesn't appear to have any defensive wounds, which would support that."

"Do you two always do this?" I asked, fascinated because what they said made sense, even though I knew it was more complicated than that. "And are you ever correct?"

Anthony looked at his grandfather, a slight smile in his eyes, but not on his lips. I sensed their bond was deep. "Pappa's family has been in the mortuary business for a few generations, going back to East Harlem, and so you learn a few things. My experience as a criminal defense lawyer also helps, but none of it is a substitute for good investigators, access to a fresh body and crime scene, and resources." He smirked. "Or magical powers."

"You're a criminal defense lawyer?" I asked.

The smirk disappeared, and both men stiffened. "Was," Anthony said tersely.

Curiosity pricked at me, but I knew better than to pry. "Your experience will still be helpful," I said. Although I still had a lot to process, I was eager to get started. There was a possibility that I could help solve a murder and bring justice to a victim' family. "So we know that the murderer was directly in front of the mayor, that the mayor didn't fight back, and that before she was shot, she and her murderer were discussing a dead woman named Bonnie."

Pappa and I began talking over each other, speculating who this woman could be and why they were discussing her, when Anthony held up a hand. "Trust me, that way madness lies," he said. "We have no way of knowing why they were discussing this woman. All we have is a name. Bonnie. That's what we start with."

"I already did," I said. "On our way here, I did an online search for Tilly Sandberg and her maiden name, Kimbleton, combined with the name Bonnie. Nothing came up. We're going to have to find ways to subtly question the people who knew her."

"The wake will be the perfect moment for me to make discreet inquiries. People are inclined to talk about their memories, and we can take it from there," Pappa began before hesitating. "But questioning the wrong people can put you and Anthony in danger. You best leave it to me."

I sliced an arm through the air. "No! I *refuse* to be sidelined again!" Pappa's eyebrows shot up and I instantly softened my tone. Respect for elders had been drilled and stuffed into me by both sides of my family, and I liked Pappa. "I'm sorry for snapping at you, but please try to understand. Today I learned I have a special gift, and I happened to find out in front of two people who are strangers to me. I can't change that. And now we're partners in trying to find out who Bonnie is, even though the only reason I'm trusting you at all is because no one would believe you if you told them what happened. But if you worry about me to the point of trying to keep me out of this, then I won't share anything new with you. I've been condescended to for years when it comes to my own parents' murders, and I can't and won't take any more of that."

Pappa made his way over to a stool and sat down with a weary sigh. "I didn't mean to be condescending. I'm sorry. Lord knows I should know better after living with Anthony for the past few months."

Anthony rolled his eyes at his grandfather before looking into mine. "I'll be blunt, Angie. I hope you keep us in the loop, and that you let us help. I'm all for justice being delivered, and these days, I don't care much how, as long as no one innocent gets hurt. But I've got too much on my plate to worry about you, and my first concerns are that you work on the mayor promptly, and you don't put my granddad in danger."

That *was* blunt, and it was exactly what this loose, short-term partnership needed. I stuck my hand out, and Anthony shook it.

"Well," Pappa said, "I'll be blunt, too, since you seem to like that." He smiled. "I'm seventy-seven years old, and what happened today was the most exciting thing that has happened to me in years. On our ride here, I realized that never once, since moving here to open my own funeral home fifty years ago, have I had anything half this exciting happen to me. I want to be a partner in this, Angie, and I can help. I've met many people through my work, made contacts everywhere, and they've all known me forever and would never suspect me of ulterior motives. We've had other murder victims here, and there are people at the sheriff's department, the fire department, and the coroner's office who like to gossip with me because I'm harmless. You may not trust me yet, but three heads are better than one."

I nodded enthusiastically, but the moment Pappa caught the look in my eye, he sobered. "But I've also learned a lot about human nature. More than I ever wanted to know. One question put to the wrong person can put us all in danger. I don't mind for myself, but you two are young, and I hope you've got a nice, long road ahead of you. I promise never to talk down to you again, but I will insist you take precautions." He held out his hand, and I shook it.

"Okay then." Anthony clapped his hands once. "This head suggests we get to work already." He turned to Pappa. "You told Brenda Mumford you'd pick up the clothes she wants her mother to wear at three, we have that funeral planning presentation at the senior center at seven, and we don't yet know how long it'll take Angie to do her part, or even if she can."

"Should I leave for this part?" I asked.

Anthony shook his head. "Pappa can tell us what he knows about Mayor Sandberg while we embalm, and you can get used to the process."

They covered themselves in white paper gowns and put on latex gloves before handing me a gown. I took it and moved to the other side of the room. I wasn't easily grossed out, but I also wasn't ready to be covered with corpse fluids.

They withdrew the blanket covering the mayor while I stared, fascinated in a way that was unfamiliar to me. As if I were a scientist rather than an artist. Utterly removed emotionally. Probably the result of trauma, but that was okay. We all of us are messed up in our way.

The mayor's mouth was open, and her skin almost translucent. Anthony proceeded to spray her mouth, nose, and eyes with a spritzer of clear liquid. "Disinfectant," Pappa told me when he caught me watching. They rubbed down her limbs, and when Anthony got ready to shoot a needle into the mayor, I looked away. Gross, I could do. Needle, I could not.

I soon realized Anthony would be doing the work, while deferring to Pappa, who looked thoughtful. "I guess I should start telling you what I know about Mayor Sandberg?" he asked after a long silence. Anthony and I both nodded. Pappa tilted his head to one side and continued to watch his grandson as he spoke. "My late wife Delfina and I knew her through various revitalization committees and organizations." I nodded because it was the same way I knew many business owners and city employees. It was also how I'd seen and heard of Pappa before, although we volunteered in different ways. "Although she was friendly, she was also very private," he continued. "The only personal information she volunteered was that she originally came here to be close to Brenda, who moved here after she married Timothy Mumford, years ago."

Mr. Mumford I knew from local billboards. "He's an estate planning attorney with Kline, Mumford, and Lorde, right?" I asked.

Pappa nodded. "People gossiped about Tilly at first, though, and that's how we found out about her reputation as a ruthless developer down in Cincinnati," he explained. "There was a rumor that Tilly married her late husband, Brenda's father, because he could help her career. He was a lot older than Tilly, and he died when Brenda was a little girl. It seems Tilly hired someone to take care of him in the end but didn't spend time with him herself.

"It all made us wary of her at first. As we got to know her, we learned she had been in a car wreck somewhere up north. She had walked away with only bruises and scratches, but it had made her question her entire life's choices.

She moved here, became active in beautifying parks and in restoring abandoned homes and was against razing condemned houses. Eight years ago, she ran for mayor for the first time, she's done a great job, everyone learned to love her, and that brings us to today."

He paused again. "Wait, no. There's that recent city council debacle about Woodruff Place. People around here are saying that could've had something to do with her murder, but I can't say I've heard about anyone involved, dead or otherwise, named Bonnie."

"Me neither. And why would they take it out on the mayor when two other council members also voted against selling it to Neil Carlson? It doesn't make sense, but we should keep it in mind." I thought about it all for a moment before remembering what he'd said at the morgue. "Can you elaborate on what you said about Brenda and her mom not having a good relationship before?"

"Brenda says they didn't reconcile until the year after Tilly moved here, but they did eventually become close."

We grew quiet for a while, each lost in their thoughts, until I asked, "Who were the mayor's closest friends?"

"Karen Schultz, Tessa Baker, and Jim Russo. Brenda requested they each read a bible verse during the ceremony. Jim Russo is also the founder of the church, or rather the organization, that Tilly has been visiting these past six months."

"I know Tessa, and I've met Mr. Russo," I said, slowly, while my mind raced ahead. Tessa lived in the Oregon District, a few blocks away from Tea and Spirits. Every year she opened her beautifully renovated gem of a house for downtown's Holiday Tour of Homes, which I always bought tickets to, and because of it, we were somewhat friendly.

Jim Russo had dropped by the mayor's office when I was doing initial sketches for the bust and had tried to tell me how to do my job. Tessa was mild-mannered and sweet and loved to gossip. Jim Russo was an opinionated blowhard who had started what he called a religious organization, House of Accountability, because he felt the co-pastor of his old church, a lovely man who everyone looked up to, was preaching too much about forgiveness.

I had never heard of Karen Schultz.

"And Brenda told you she and Tilly had reconciled, which means they had a falling out at some point. Did she tell you what happened?" I prompted him next.

"That's all she said." Pappa shrugged one shoulder. "People reminisce out loud throughout this process, without even realizing it, and some, like her, are then apologetic, thinking you've heard it all before, even when we don't mind and understand." He looked up at the clock then and winced. "Oh my. Will you look at the time! I don't think I'll make it to Brenda's at three." His lips pressed together in a tight frown. "I'll have to give her a call and see if it's okay if I stop by later."

It was clear it distressed him to break his word. And I had a solution to that. "I can go in your place. I can say you sent me because I need to know how she wants her mom's hair and makeup done. Maybe she'll start reminiscing with me, too." I tried to keep my eagerness out of my voice.

He hesitated. "I want to trust you, Angie, the way you want to trust us. But I can't have you focusing on Bonnie so much that you start digging to deeply and upset her. Her feelings have to come first."

Impulsively, I grabbed his hand. "I swear to you I won't upset her. I've been on the other end of nosy, insensitive rumormongers. I don't have it in me to upset someone that way."

Pappa studied me a long moment before nodding once. "All right. I'll allow it. I'll text you her address and let her know you'll be there instead of me."

"Yes! Thank you for trusting me with this!" I exclaimed.

Brenda Mumford lived at Performance Place. If I left now, I had just enough time to walk to my house, let my dog out to do his business, and grab my car, which I hardly ever used. I wished I didn't have to use it now…

I had inherited my dad's old, beloved, lime green Honda s2000. Sometimes I thought my parents were in Heaven; sometimes I believed we were all stuck in *The Matrix*. Sometimes I was convinced we're all allowed as many lives as we need until we get it right, and still other times I despaired this life was it. But if there *was* a Heaven and my dad *was* there, he has cried at every scratch I've accidentally put on his car.

One day, I'd have it restored.

I turned to give Pappa a reassuring smile on my way out the door and caught a dark look pass between him and Anthony.

As I walked up the driveway, I thought about that look. Midway up, I stopped. Pappa and Anthony needed money, and Anthony believed a successful wake and funeral for someone as popular as Mayor Sandberg could bring them new clients. Her prepaid funeral plan was through them. "What if Pappa or Anthony is the killer?" I wondered.

"Nobody's ever suspected me of anything half so interesting before!" Pappa said behind me. I jumped, both startled and embarrassed, and then turned to see a bright eyed Pappa chuckling.

"I'm sorry," I said, feeling mortified. "Sorting complicated thoughts out loud is a bad habit of mine. I didn't mean anything by it."

"It's okay, Angie. This is all new. It's smart to suspect everyone," he said. "I came after you because we realized I'll only need Anthony's steady hand for about fifteen more minutes and then he can go with you." I narrowed my eyes at him and Pappa clucked his tongue. "Don't give me that look! It's not that we don't trust you. But Anthony can answer questions Brenda might have about the wake and funeral, and he has experience with criminal investigations. He might catch something you miss. More heads are better than one and all that, remember?"

So that was the dark look I'd caught… Anthony thought he could do a better job than me. I folded my arms across my chest. "I'm sorry, but I can't wait for him. I have to go home and walk my dog first."

"Why don't you borrow the minivan, then?" he suggested. "I don't mind you driving it as long as you have insurance. And

Anthony can take his motorcycle and meet you at Brenda's." He soft pitched the keys to the van, and I caught them, deciding it was in everyone's interest that I surrender gracefully this time. We needed to build trust. It would be good for Anthony to see that I wouldn't say or do anything to jeopardize their business relationship with Brenda.

"We'll get started on reconstruction as soon as you get back," Pappa shot over his shoulder as he turned to leave, and I felt a shiver of excitement that I hadn't felt in a long time. I wondered what was wrong with me, that I was looking forward to re-sculpting the dead. Maybe I had been a mummifier in another life, back in Egyptian times, with my cousin Wanda, who insisted she was one of Cleopatra's handmaidens who'd committed suicide with her.

I climbed into the minivan, grateful to be saved a hot and sweaty ten-minute walk to my house. Along the way I went over every conversation I'd had with Tilly Sandberg, to see if there was something I could use to get Brenda Mumford to open up and share more about her mom.

When I got home, I was greeted by my one true love: a fluffy beagle Yorkshire terrier mix. Ears, tricolor, and size were beagle; bark, fluff, and nose were Yorkshire terrier. Tito Bendito was always as happy to see me as I was to see him. I could tell him all about my day while he wagged his tail and smiled (whoever said that dogs don't smile, that they just bared their teeth, had never met Tito Bendito). I kneeled in front of him, looked deep into his eyes, told him that I was a Magical Gomez after all, and not sure how I felt about it. He put his front paws on my shoulders and looked at me like he understood what I was going through. We hugged, walked out so he could do his business, and I was off again.

Anthony was waiting for me by the front door of Brenda's apartment building. He nodded a greeting and said, "You do the talking."

"Really?" I raised an eyebrow. "I thought that's why you insisted on coming along, so you could do the talking."

He quirked a smile. "I don't trust as easily as Pappa does and I want to make sure you don't alienate our client. But I think she'll respond better to you than to me." He opened the door and motioned for me to go first. The doorman called up, and soon Brenda Mumford was ushering us into the living room of her trendy apartment. A light blue sofa and two white fabric armchairs surrounded a coffee table. On top of the coffee table was an envelope, a photo album, and a few pictures strewn about. A garment bag was draped over one of the armchairs.

Brenda gestured to the sofa and Anthony and I sat down next to each other, while Brenda chose the empty armchair.

The conversation flowed more smoothly than I had anticipated. It brought her peace to talk about how she wanted her mother's hair and makeup for the wake. But it was hard to keep my eyes on her when I was dying to look at the pictures and album on the table. My mind searched for a way to ask to see them. When there was a lull, Anthony gestured to it and asked, "Are you searching for pictures to display during the wake?"

"I had already chosen a few I think she would like," she said, indicating the envelope on the table. "But then I found an album I had never seen before in mom's attic. I've been looking through it."

"I'd like to get a better sense of her. Is it alright if I look at some her pictures?" I asked after a moment. Out of the corner of my eye I saw Anthony give a slight nod of approval.

Brenda slid the album my way. "Of course."

I carefully flipped through the pages while Brenda asked Anthony's opinion on the photos she was thinking of displaying at the wake. When I got to the last page, I observed a tiny corner of a picture sticking out behind another one. I showed this to Brenda, and she took the album from me to peel the protective film away from the page.

"What an eye you have," she marveled as she carefully lifted the first picture away. It revealed a black and white picture of two toddler girls. One was plump and adorable. The other, who looked to be about six months younger, was so emaciated, she was painful to look at.

Brenda let out a gasp. "Oh, will you look at that!"

"Is one of them your mom?" I asked.

"This one must be," she said, pointing to the plump toddler and smiling. "See the birthmark on top of her head? She hated it, but several prominent dermatologists told her it couldn't be removed. It was silly because you couldn't even see it. But wanting to look her best was the one thing about her that never changed." Her smile faltered.

"Do you know who the other girl is?" Anthony asked in a gentle tone.

Brenda shook her head. "My mom was abandoned as an infant, and she grew up in an orphanage somewhere in upstate New York. Probably it's another orphan." She shrugged. "She never talked about her youth, except to always tell me how lucky I was when I was younger." Her gaze became unfocused. "This must be her only baby picture. I asked her for one once when we did an ancestry project in high school. Not that she would've helped me back then, but I did comb through everything in the house and didn't find any, so I figured she was telling the truth."

The picture became limp in her hand, and I noticed there was something written in a corner on the back. I pointed it out to her, and she flipped it over.

"Tilly and Bonnie, Scarsdale Orphan's Home, and then a date, but I can't make it out."

Bonnie!

FOUR

Bonnie.

My heart slammed against my chest so hard it made me lightheaded. It took every ounce of willpower I possessed to calm down.

Brenda peered into Anthony's face and asked, "Are you all right?"

I glanced at him, too. It was as if he'd been turned to stone. I was tempted to poke him. "I'm fine," he let out. "It's just very touching to see you make a new discovery."

"And what a sweet one it is." I swallowed. "Do you know if your mom and Bonnie kept in touch?"

Brenda stared at the picture. "I wouldn't know—I've never heard of her. But I guess it's possible."

Anthony cleared his throat. "Growing up in an orphanage must've been tough. Do you know how long your mom was there?" Somehow, it didn't sound intrusive coming from him. His demeanor was too reserved to come off as nosy.

"I don't know. Mom rarely spoke about the past," she answered, her face expressionless.

Pappa's warnings about upsetting his client echoed in my head. But there was a huge clue to a murder right in front of our noses! We couldn't let it go without trying to learn more.

I racked my brain for a considerate way to dig deeper. All I could think of was that I always appreciated it when people told me stories about my parents. With that in mind, I leaned forward and shared, "Your mom was always focused on the here and now. I enjoyed listening to her talk about the city's potential, and all the projects she had going on. Only once did she ever mention anything about her past."

Brenda tilted her head. "Really? What did she say?"

"I asked her once if she wanted to see the sketch of her that I had finished, but she told me that she never liked looking at herself, because it reminded her of lost time." This was true, but I wasn't sure where I was going with it. I'd have to wing it. "I don't remember her exact words after that, but it sounded like she had experienced tragedy growing up. Maybe that's why she never spoke about the orphanage or her friends there."

After a long moment Brenda shrugged and repeated, "Like I said, she never talked about it." She let the picture fall onto the table and began to get up. "I'm expecting company soon but thank you for stopping by."

Anthony and I stood up, too. He caught my eye and subtly glanced at his phone and then at the picture of Tilly and Bonnie on the coffee table.

The last thing I wanted to do was trouble Brenda any further. But Anthony wanted to take a picture of the photo of Tilly and Bonnie, and it was a good idea. "Thanks for seeing us," I said before pausing, putting my hand to my temple, and crumpling back onto the sofa.

"Angie!" Brenda exclaimed. Anthony knelt in front of me and asked, "Are you all right?"

"I—I dehydrate easily, and I haven't had anything to drink since you picked me up this morning," I explained before turning to Brenda. "I hate to trouble you, but all I need is a cool glass of water and I'll be fine."

"Of course. It's a hot and humid day, and I'm grateful you agreed to work on my mother on such short notice." Her calm, even tone was back as she walked to the refrigerator, but the open concept floor plan made it so she could see us from the kitchen.

She brought me the glass of water, asked a few questions about how I was feeling, and after they both made sure I was okay, I got up again. "Thank you for your time. I'm sorry to have caused you any concern." I picked up the garment bag with Tilly Sandberg's clothes, and Brenda gave Anthony the envelope with the pictures she wanted displayed.

"Thank you for agreeing to help Pappa," she repeated as we left.

Anthony and I didn't speak until we reached the elevator. "Bonnie," I said.

"Don't even..." Anthony leaned against the wall and looked toward the ceiling. "My mind is officially blown. I was starting to wonder if you were crazy and had pulled us all into your delusion."

"Me too," I agreed, not in the least bit offended. "Did you get the picture?"

"I think so." He glanced at his phone. "She kept peeking at us from the kitchen. I was only able to take a quick shot when she put the jug of water back in the fridge." I leaned over to look at the pic. It was blurry. "I'm not sure how much help it would be even if it was clear, but it seemed like a good idea to have a copy."

I agreed. "Send it to me when you get a chance."

We arrived on the ground floor, the elevator doors began to slide open and I caught sight of Lillian Carlson just outside the front door of the building. "That's Neil Carlson's wife," I whispered to Anthony after doing a double take. I had never seen her dressed so casually. Grey, untucked T shirt, large sunglasses, ankle jeans, sneakers, no makeup, and a baseball cap over a low bun. The only reason I knew it was her was because of the flawless symmetry of her face. A classic square with perfectly aligned cheekbones and jawline, and proportionate features.

"Neil Carlson? The developer who pressured Tilly to vote to raze the Woodruff building?" Anthony asked out of the side of his mouth as we stepped from the elevator into the lobby. I gave him a quick nod and we were silent as the doorman opened the door for her. Lillian gave me a quick glance as she swept by us but stepped into the elevator without acknowledging me. She and I had met, but she was the type to look past you and pretend she didn't know you if you weren't important enough.

"What if she's the visitor Brenda was expecting?" I wondered out loud. "That would be odd, wouldn't it, when her husband waged such an intense public campaign against Mayor Sandberg before the vote?"

"Maybe. Or maybe she lives here. The doorman didn't ask her where she was going," Anthony pointed out.

I considered it. "She lives in Oakwood, but it's possible they keep an apartment here as well." I had lived in Dayton for close to seventeen years, and for as long as I could remember, the Carlson's had been among the wealthiest and most involved citizens in the region. They lived on an estate in an affluent, inner ring suburb and hosted many events there. Mrs. Carlson was in her late forties but looked a decade younger, an elegant, poised blond with a practiced smile meant to intimidate rather than invite you closer.

"Let's wait and see if the elevator stops at Brenda's floor," Anthony suggested with a shrug. "It might not mean anything if she does, but we're trying to learn more about Tilly Sandberg's life. Any small detail could be a piece of the larger puzzle." He opened a map on his phone and pretended to discuss the best route to a brewery, so the doorman wouldn't suspect us of loitering for no reason. I played along, until the lighted numbers atop the elevator told us Lillian had stopped on the floor before Brenda's.

Anthony sighed. "Let's not waste any more time. You've got work to do, and we need to tell Pappa about Bonnie."

I followed Anthony out of the parking lot, but while his motorcycle allowed him to weave through traffic, I got stuck behind a dump truck.

When I walked into the embalming room, Pappa was sitting on a stool in front of Anthony, his face looking like the "mind-blown" emoji, only oval and not round. I folded my arms across my chest and looked at Anthony. "Really? You couldn't wait for me to get here before you told him?"

"No. I really couldn't," he answered with a grin.

Pappa looked at me. "Bonnie is real. Or was."

"Yes! And it feels wrong to have this crucial piece of information and not go to the police with it." This had been foremost on my mind on the way back.

Pappa sighed. "I agree… but how do we reveal what we know?"

"An anonymous tip?" I suggested.

Anthony shook his head. "They'd need context, and we have no way of giving it to them. We'd have to say we overheard it, and that could derail the investigation. They'd start looking for this anonymous tipster as a possible witness."

I stopped to look at them. "What do we do then? We can't just do nothing."

"Tell me more about Bonnie," Pappa said. "Let's see how much we can figure out ourselves."

I nodded. "She looked younger than Tilly, and she was painfully thin. They were both at Scarsdale Orphanage as infants."

Anthony went to the laptop in the corner. "I'll look up the orphanage and the years around when Tilly Sandberg was born along with the name Bonnie. I'm good at finding information quickly."

Pappa turned in the stool to gaze down at Tilly. "It sounds like Tilly and the murderer were having a conversation or argument over a dead person named Bonnie who was at the orphanage with Tilly."

I tilted my head to look down at her, too. "If we can find out when Bonnie died, we might have a place to start."

After a while, Anthony blew out a frustrated breath. "All I can find is an article saying that Scarsdale was closed fifty-three years ago. It also looks like someone started a forum to reunite people who grew up there, but only three have responded and none of them is named Bonnie. Absolutely nothing else comes up.

I sighed, too. "And Brenda completely closed up on us. I don't think we can approach her again with this."

Pappa considered us. "I can ask others during the wake, but we'll have to figure out a safe way to bring the name up. Normally I could say someone named Bonnie called about sending flowers, but if this Bonnie person is dead, then that's not going to help."

"You can bring up the picture," I said to him. "And talk about how nice it was that Brenda was able to find it."

"That's an idea," he said. "I guess I could say you and Anthony told me about it, since I didn't see it myself." He didn't look convinced.

I turned to Anthony. "You didn't show him the picture?"

Pappa perked up. "Brenda gave you the old picture? To display?" he asked. "Why didn't you say so before? That will make it easier to bring up Bonnie." He held his hand out for the picture.

"Um. No. Anthony took a picture of the old photo when Brenda went to the kitchen to get some water. It's on his phone," I explained.

Pappa turned to Anthony. "You snuck a picture that belonged to our client when our client's back was turned to you?" he asked, his voice low.

Anthony's throat worked. "It, uh, seemed like a smart idea at the time. Because we're trying to solve a murder, and all."

Pappa slowly and silently made his way over to the desk, slid a heavy book titled *The Funeral Professional's Ultimate Guide to Extraordinary Customer Service* off the shelf, and shoved it into Anthony's chest. "Take that upstairs and re-read the chapter on empathy and respect. When Angie and I are done, you and I will discuss it at length." He turned to me. "Angie, you and I will get to work. When we're done, you can take the book home and read it, too. We'll have no more talk of Bonnie tonight. We're not gonna solve anything right now and we have a job to do."

"Yes, Pappa."

Pappa and I worked for three hours. He instructed me on the use of mortuary wax, plastina, molding clay, and plaster of Paris, but I was proud to see I needed little direction. He answered my questions but didn't once intrude to correct anything I was doing. In a way, it felt like I had been doing it forever. He was also good, quiet, solid company. I needed it because I heard *Bonnie is dead* so many times while I worked that I grew used to it and it calmed me to analyze the way it was said. The *Bonnie* was shaky, the *is* was emphasized, and the *dead* was final. "What do you think it means?" I asked Pappa when I told him. "It almost sounds like she's trying to convince whoever she was talking to that this Bonnie person really was dead."

Pappa stared at the mayor for a long time before shaking his head. "Everything I can think of sounds like the plot of a thriller, and not like real life. For instance, maybe Tilly was supposed to kill Bonnie for some reason and didn't, and the murderer found out. Or maybe Bonnie wasn't really dead, and she had something on Tilly and the murderer. But the murderer found out she wasn't dead, and Tilly didn't believe it." He lifted his hands to show the impossibility of guessing.

It all sounded too much like a telenovela, I acknowledged, but that only encouraged me to consider even more fantastical ideas in my head.

As I thought, I worked with a different kind of care. I loved sketching and sculpting, but I loved them for myself, to express my worldview. Sculpting busts became a career of sorts after I won a contest during college. It was one of a few ways I now eked out a living as an artist. It was also the least satisfying. I was deeply fortunate to have been left an estate valued at two hundred grand by my parents, which had left me with no college debt, and the knowledge that money quite easily disappeared. It was now invested in mutual funds. My mother's mom, Abuela Nydia, despaired that I didn't major in a subject that would have set me up for life. Abuela Luci was initially proud I'd adjusted to a simple lifestyle and had followed what she thought was my bliss, but she now sensed that had never quite been the case.

When we were done, Pappa looked at me in wonder. "You're a genius." My heart swelled with the feeling that I was part of something bigger than me. A way for others to find a measure of peace. To see a person one last time and feel connected enough to who they were in life to issue a true final goodbye. "You've earned every penny."

That got my attention, and I was shocked to realize I had never asked how many pennies. The idea that Brenda Mumford had requested me, that it wouldn't take me long, and the discovery that *I hear dead people* had dominated my thoughts. "And how much is that exactly?" I asked.

"Well, your skills are the best I've seen, and professionals of your caliber charge four hundred dollars an hour. So, for today, one thousand two hundred, if I'm to be fair, and I could be no less."

My eyes bugged and my jaw dropped. Pappa went to call Brenda Mumford and tell her that she had been right about me, and I plopped down on the stool he'd vacated.

My current fee for sculpting worked out to about one-tenth the amount Pappa had quoted. I wasn't well-known anywhere except Dayton, and even here, it was more through word of mouth and networking. I also taught workshops to seniors and disadvantaged kids, through grant collaboratives, and that worked out to minimum wage, but I loved teaching those two groups too much to ever give it up.

When Pappa came back five minutes later, I was still marveling at my newfound largess. "Anthony and I have that advanced funeral planning presentation to get to. Would you like to stay and work on the mayor's hair and makeup? I think you can handle it on your own."

"Yes! I'd like that."

"All right then. Just turn the lock on that door behind you before you leave if you decide to go home before we get back," he instructed, pointing to the back door. "You can keep the minivan until tomorrow, so you don't have to walk if it gets too dark. I'll take the hearse."

Anthony and Pappa left and I began working on Tilly Sandberg's hair, snipping a little over an inch off a silver curl to get it to caress her chin below her lip, the way it did in life, the bust I'd sculpted, and the pictures Brenda had given us. I stepped back to check my work, and that was when it hit me.

There was no birthmark on Mayor Sandberg's head.

FIVE

He who seeks, finds.

SPANISH AND LATIN AMERICAN PROVERB

Stunned stupid, I got as far away from the mayor as possible so I could think.

What if Brenda was wrong about the birthmark?

No. It made no sense that a daughter would remember a distinctive birthmark that *wasn't* there. It would be more likely for her to forget a birthmark that had once been there.

Maybe the mayor had removed her birthmark later, with new technology? That was it. She hated it and never gave up. I sat down in front of the laptop Pappa kept in the far-left corner of the room and searched for red, raised birthmarks until I found one identical to the one I'd seen on the baby, and then researched its removal. What I read gave me pause. I checked my phone to see if Anthony had sent me the picture of the photograph. He had.

I opened it, zoomed in, and studied every detail. The longer I did so, the more certainty and dread I felt.

I shut the laptop and tried to bring order to my racing thoughts. I now had information that possibly no one else had. What was the right thing to do? As much as I wanted to wait for Pappa and Anthony to come back, a sense of responsibility made me keep moving forward without them. This wasn't about me discovering I was a Magical Gomez or about trying to solve the strange Bonnie puzzle. This was about Mayor Sandberg's *murder*. And evidence belonged in the hands of detectives.

But *did* I have evidence? I needed more proof than "I've got a good eye, and I did an internet search" before I went to the authorities.

I grabbed my messenger bag. The next logical step was to talk to the mayor's current hairstylist. Tessa would be able to tell me who that was. Ten minutes later, I was knocking on Tessa Baker's front door.

"Why, Angie! What a surprise! Come in," she began the moment she opened the door. "How is your grandmother?" she asked as she led me into her cozy living room. She offered me a seat, and I took the only one not full of knitting yarn, cats, or an excess of throw pillows. Her living room was all flowered upholstery, walnut furniture, and bric-a-brac.

"She's great! Thank you for asking."

"Would you like some coffee or tea?" Anticipation was coming off her in waves, and I knew she was as eager as I was to get pleasantries out of the way.

"No, thank you."

I was about to tell her my reason for visiting when she leaned in, eyes wide. "I heard you agreed to restore Tilly. Brenda was so grateful. It's very good of you. How *is* Tilly doing?"

I blinked at that. After a moment's thought, I offered, "She's, uh, looking like herself again."

"Were you able to, um, fix the face wounds?"

"Yes. She looks good as new." I patted Tessa's hand. "And that's why I'm here. Her face is beautiful like we all remember, but we would like to know the best technique for taming her waves and curls. Can you tell me who her hairstylist was?"

"Oh, I'm so glad to hear that! I'd like to have a moment with her, but I wasn't sure I could manage it. A closed casket isn't the same, you know, but I also couldn't say goodbye to her in an open casket if I felt I wouldn't see her the way I remembered her. And Tilly was very particular about her hair! As am I." Her eyes widened as if she'd had an idea. "You should take care of me, too, when my time comes."

I smiled. "That's a long way off, Mrs. Baker. Maybe we can talk about it in twenty years?"

"Very well." She chuckled before becoming somber and shaking her head. "Poor Tilly," she said on a sigh. After a long moment, she gathered herself and looked at me again. "Her hairstylist was Maddie Lentil, on Jones Street. Tilly's been seeing her for twelve years or so, ever since she moved here. I'm sure she'll know what tools and products to use."

Twelve years. Pappa had said that's when she'd had that accident that inspired her to turn over a new leaf.

"Do you know who did her hair before Maddie Lentil?" I asked.

Tessa Baker leaned in, her eyes sparkling with the promise of an interesting tidbit. "Well, I once heard that Lillian Carlson used to drive all the way to Cincinnati to do Tilly's hair, back when Tilly lived there. That's not something I can imagine Lillian doing, can you?"

"No. Not at all." My belly did a flip flop. Why would Lillian agree to drive to Cincinnati? And why would Tilly switch stylists after she moved here when her old stylist was now closer than before?

Tessa gave me an odd look then. "But that was a long time ago, and I don't think it would help to talk to her. Especially when she and her husband were mad at Tilly over that vote. Why do you ask?"

"Well," I began, thinking fast, "I've had the same hairstylist for years, and we've become friends. To leave her would feel like a breakup. I guess hearing that Mayor Sandberg switched made me wonder if it had something to do with her move here, but I guess it didn't, since Lillian Carlson lives here, too."

"Oh, I know exactly what you mean! I've been with Izzy down on Wayne for years, and she would find out if I ever switched to another local person. I could never hurt her like that. She's become one of my best friends, listening to me chat while she does my hair. I tell her she could've been a therapist."

"I think everyone feels that way about their hairstylist." I leaned toward her and smiled as if we were close friends sharing some harmless gossip. "But I didn't know Lillian Carlson was *working* as a hairstylist twelve years ago. She was already married to Neil."

Tessa seemed to think about it before shrugging and saying, "Maybe it was a favor for an old friend."

It was a definite possibility, and I doubted Tessa had any other theories to offer. We chatted a bit more about how sad and shocking the murder was, and when we both grew silent at the magnitude of it all, I decided it was time to leave. I squeezed her hand, told her I was sorry for her loss, and we said our goodbyes.

I stood on the sidewalk and stared into space. All I needed to find out before I went to detectives was if there was a possibility that the birthmark had been there sometime during the last twelve years, so I could give them enough information to take me seriously.

Maddie Lentil was flipping the open sign to the closed side when I drove up. Our eyes met, and I held up one finger and smiled to indicate I only needed a quick moment of her time.

"I won't hold you up! I just need a few pointers on how to style Tilly Sandberg's hair," I said after she opened the salon door and I explained I was working on the mayor.

"Oh. Sure. Anything for Tilly. What do you need to know?"

"Well…." I had come up with a plan to suss her out on the birthmark in the short time it had taken me to drive here, but it depended on Maddie knowing as little about dead bodies as I did. "There's a mark on her scalp that I'm not sure is due to a birthmark, or a particular discoloration that occurs on thin skin during rigor mortis. If it's a birthmark, I don't want to cover it with makeup, because it's a part of her." I studied Maddie closely as I said all this and saw no change whatsoever in her expression when I mentioned the birthmark.

"She didn't have a birthmark, so it makes sense to cover it up. I know it brings comfort to people to view their loved ones as they remembered them." Her words and reaction betrayed nothing but sincere interest, so I went to the second part of my plan.

"I agree, but it's all so new to me. I've been reading up to make sure I get everything right, and some mourners prefer to see the deceased the way they looked most of their life. Tessa Baker mentioned that Lillian Carlson had been her hairstylist before you. Did you two ever talk about your approach to Tilly's hair?"

That made Maddie give me an odd but still friendly look. "No…Lillian and I don't exactly run around in the same circles, but you should probably ask Brenda what she prefers for her mom."

I nodded. "I've been trying to avoid burdening her with details, but I see I'll have to. I was surprised to learn that Lillian Carlson did Tilly's hair for so long, but I'm glad it's you now because I'm not friendly enough with Lillian to approach her. I only know her through civic events involving art."

We chatted for a few more minutes, trying to sound as if we weren't gossiping even though we were, but I didn't get any new information, and in truth, I didn't need it. I had enough.

"I can't believe I'll never see her again. For twelve years, every six weeks on a Monday, half an inch off, like clockwork." Maddie smiled reminiscing. "She was a good listener, too. Usually, it's the other way around—clients want to chat while I listen. But Tilly liked to ask me about my life, and she always had good advice."

I agreed because it had been the same with me, even though I hadn't spent as much time with her. We said our goodbyes, and soon I was at the sheriff's department, where it had all started three days before, hoping to see Sergeant Beemer, the detective in charge.

But Derick Hugo was the only one in the bullpen. He and I had gone out on two dates a few months back, hadn't felt the magic, but we were still friendly.

"Hi Angie," he said, looking wary. News of my last visit must've spread.

"Hello to you." I gave him a bright smile. "I'm here to speak to Sergeant Beemer about something totally unrelated to my parents."

He nodded. "She's not here, but if its department related, I can take down your information. If not, I can give you some pen and paper and you can leave a note on her desk." I looked into his eyes. There was some hesitancy behind the friendliness. I wondered what, exactly, had been said to him about my last visit.

I cleared my throat. "Who else is working on Mayor Sandberg's case?"

"Why?"

"I might have relevant information, *that's* why."

He gave me a look, and I returned it. "Is this like the relevant information you told Benny Rover you had the other day?"

Aha. So, word had spread. And my reign on my temper began to falter. I had thought that Mahoney wouldn't tell anybody about my tactics. Didn't I deserve some patience and understanding when it came to my parents? The department certainly believed they were entitled to patience. Years of it!

I tried to unclench my jaw so I could fake-smile again. "No. This is different."

He leaned back. "Run it by me."

I took a deep breath and thought. Derrick was in the Special Victims Unit, and presumably, I could tell him. But when I thought about my suspicions, I couldn't help but doubt myself. I gave him an imploring look. "Look, Derrick, you've worked here long enough to know that I don't normally go around sticking my nose into the sheriff's department's business. In fact, nobody has ever seen me here for anything other than my parents' case. But today I was tasked with reconstructing Mayor Sandberg, and I've never done anything like it. I think I may have spotted something, but I might be wrong. If I am, I don't want that broadcast, and I now see you all broadcast everything around here. I'd rather share my information with the lead detective on the case."

"Is it because you turned me down for a third date, and you think I'll hold it against you by not taking you seriously?"

What?

He dropped his chair back down from its hind legs with a thump. "Because I'm not upset with you, Angie. Everyone warned me exactly what would happen. That I might get a second date, but that you don't do thirds. There are no hard feelings." He folded his hands in front of him on the desk, a picture of professionalism. "You can give me the information you have on the case, and I'll pass it along if it's relevant. I promise."

It took all I had not to shake him. Or question him. Who, exactly, was "everyone" who had warned him about me? Before I could decide which to do, a sharp voice cut across the room. "Miss Gomez Gomez, what case do you have information on?"

We both turned to Lieutenant Mahoney's door. It was the first time I had seen him look anything other than calm and cool, or amused. And boy, was he not amused. His blue eyes were blazing like twin blue flames, making me inexplicably feel like confessing everything I'd ever done wrong—no wonder he'd been named managing supervisor at a relatively young age.

"I'm here about Mayor Sandberg's case," I blurted.

He motioned me into his office with his head. "Sergeant Beemer's not here, but I'm supervising the case."

I suppose I should have been happy that the incident from the other day didn't have him turning me away, but he was looking formidable, and I hoped I wasn't about to waste his time.

Instead of sitting behind his desk, he leaned on its edge and gestured to the chair in front of him. I had read somewhere that standing over a person was a power move, so I remained standing. But his gaze was intense, and I knew I had to get down to business. Where to start…?

The beginning. Leaving out the small detail that I could hear a dead person's last thoughts. I nodded once in a decisive manner. "You were close this morning when you guessed I was at the morgue to consult about Mayor Sandberg. Brenda Mumford asked me to restore her mother's face." His eyebrows lifted at that, but he didn't say a word. "I decided I could do it, but before I began working on her, I stopped at Brenda's house on an errand for Mr. Pappalardo. Brenda was leafing through a picture album she had found, and when she turned a page, I saw something peeking out of the back of a photograph. She peeled it away, and we saw it was a picture of Mayor Sandberg as a toddler, along with another girl. Brenda had never seen it before. The names Bonnie and Tilly and a date were written on the back. Brenda told me that her mom grew up in an orphanage, that she didn't know anything about her mom's time there, and that she'd never heard of a Bonnie. The thing is…"

This is where I doubted myself.

"Go on," he said, his voice gentle now.

I met his eyes, and they had softened. It gave me the encouragement I needed to continue. "I'm certain now that the toddlers were identical twins. I don't think Brenda realized it, though, and I didn't realize it until later."

His silence was heavy enough that I knew I'd surprised him, even when his expression revealed nothing. "How can you be sure they were identical twins if Brenda didn't notice and if it wasn't immediately clear to you?" he asked.

I began to pace to help me find the words I needed in English only. Sometimes, when I was nervous or excited, words came to me in a mix of English and Spanish—Spanglish. It wouldn't do to tell him that Anthony had snuck a picture of the photograph. It would seem like an odd thing to do and Mahoney would want to know why. I'd have to find another way to explain it.

After a moment, I hit on a way of explaining it that also held the truth. "When something captures my attention, I stop seeing the whole, and instead I see—or rather I scan—lines, curves, shapes, colors, shadows, contours, and even spaces. The toddlers captured my attention, but I didn't interpret what I'd scanned until later. There are lots of details that can make a person's features look different from one moment to the next, but I understand those details, and how to adjust for them. One toddler was painfully thin, slouched over, and looked sickly, which changed their contours, color, and more. It's also harder to adjust for babies, but I did, and I have no doubt they were identical twins."

I stopped to study his reaction. His eyes were on me, but he wasn't looking at me. The wheels in his head were turning. "There's more." His eyes refocused on me at that, and he nodded for me to continue. I took a deep breath. "One of the toddlers, the healthy-looking one, had a dark red, raised birthmark on the right side of her head. That's how Brenda said she knew which baby her mother was. She spoke about how much her mom hated her birthmark, and the lengths she took to cover it up. I looked up the birthmark, and I know the internet isn't always reliable, but website after website stated it was one of those rare ones that can't be removed."

For the first time since I'd first spoken to Brian a few days ago, I had an inkling to what he was feeling. He had frozen, and his widened eyes were fixed on mine. His reaction made it all finally seem real, and the full weight of it came down on me. "From your reaction, I think you know that the Tilly Sandberg I'm working on does not have a birthmark," I said.

Brian gave me a cautious nod. "Our coroner is detailed and thorough. After spending the week looking through past files, I'm familiar with her work. She would have noted a birthmark in her initial report, and she didn't." He spoke in a mechanical way, and I gathered he was processing what I'd told him against whatever information he already had, while also keeping me here until he finished thinking everything though. I doubted he'd let me go out into the world with potentially explosive information without first giving me a warning.

Finally, he straightened and focused on me again. "Don't hold back any other thoughts, Angie, like any observations you made while talking to Brenda, or looking at her pictures, or anything, no matter how silly you think it is."

Bonnie is dead. I looked away before I could stop myself, which was, of course, a notoriously suspicious move, so I pretended I was focusing on the chair and thinking. "There's a lot of circumstantial evidence that the Tilly Sandberg of the last twelve years wasn't who she said she was…"

"Go on."

"I'm sure you already know that everyone says she turned over a new leaf twelve years ago, after her accident up north. Well, she switched hairstylists twelve years ago, too." I met his eyes again. "I know you know where I've been going with all this. Maybe it wasn't because she was starting over. Maybe she came back a different person because she *was* a different person. She was Bonnie." Feeling excited that the truth seemed to be unraveling, I began to pace again. "And Tessa Baker told me that Tilly's old hairstylist was Lillian Carlson! Why was she doing Tilly Sandberg's hair? It could be because they were friends and it was a special favor, especially if Tilly was particular about her hair, but isn't it odd that no one liked Tilly back then and that she had no known friends, and yet this one particular person who didn't need to work would do her hair for her?" I turned around abruptly and saw Brian's expression had gone blank again. "What?" I demanded.

"When and why did you talk to Tessa Baker about this?"

"Before coming here. I didn't trust what my brain was trying to tell me because it seemed too crazy, and I didn't want to waste your time. I needed more evidence. I decided to pretend that I wanted to know who Mayor Sandberg's hairstylist was so I could get their opinion on styling her hair. The fact that she switched stylists twelve years ago was too much of a coincidence. It was clear the *new* Tilly didn't want to explain how her birthmark disappeared. I decided I had enough information to come to you."

He pushed off the desk, saying, "Fair enough," with an exaggerated sigh that told me to keep the fact that I also spoke to Maddie Lentil to myself. For now, at least. "Anything else?" he asked.

The image of Lillian walking into Brenda's building came back to me. "Well… Maybe. Anthony and I spotted Mrs. Carlson at Performance Place earlier today. We waited to see if she was going to visit Brenda, but she stopped on the floor below hers. The doorman let her in, as if she lived there." I shrugged, aware that it wasn't much. "I'm only mentioning it since her name came up as Tilly's old hairdresser."

He looked outside his window for a long moment before turning back to me.

"Can you tell me if Brenda has an alibi?" I asked.

He studied me before nodding and saying, "Yes. She was at an Urban Renewal convention in Columbus, and it was recorded as it was streamed live. Why?"

I lifted one shoulder. "I guess a part of me wonders if she wanted me to find that picture. I mean, first, she requests me, specifically, to work on her mom, and then that picture just happens to be sticking out while I'm there?"

He gave me a long, considering look. "I'll keep that in mind."

"Are we done?" I asked.

"No. But I'll walk you to your car."

"Why?"

"I'll tell you when we get to your car."

I let out my own exasperated sigh, and it was much better than his. The man liked to call the shots and not be questioned. It was aggravating. We passed a few people who said goodnight before Brian was stopped by someone requesting a signature. Derrick Hugo took the opportunity to pull me aside and ask if we were good. "I'm seeing someone, and you know her, so I don't want you to think I said what I said because I'm upset about us not working out. It just bothered me that you didn't trust me to do my job."

"I do trust you to do your job. As I said, I didn't trust the validity of my information, and I don't want my credibility here completely shot." He nodded but still didn't look convinced. Time for a change of subject. "Who are you seeing, and who exactly did you mean by 'everyone' when you said 'everyone' warned you about me?"

He smiled. "Ashley Krueger. And 'everyone' was only Brandon Downes."

"Brandon Downes and I went out *exactly* once in college, and he knows *exactly* nothing about me! And I haven't seen Ashley in ages, but I like her, and I can totally see you two together," I gushed. We began walking to the door and left Brian behind. Let him catch up. He did. Derrick opened the door for us and said goodbye.

When Brian and I stepped outside, I turned to him. "Why do you want to finish talking to me outside? Is your upcoming warning for me to keep my mouth shut about Tilly Sandberg going to involve threats in a dark corner of the parking lot, for ambiance?"

The corner of his mouth lifted. "Not yet. As long as you leave the detective work to the detectives." Before I could protest, he moved on. "I walked you out so that people here take you seriously again. If they see me walking out with you after you came in saying you had evidence, they will."

My eyes narrowed. "Right. I almost forgot about that. Were you the one who told everyone I was bluffing about having new evidence the other day? Because I expected, and believe I deserve, a little something called empathy from you."

"It wasn't me."

"Who told them, Captain Webber?"

He smiled a disarming smile that made him look like he was flirting even though I knew he was not. It was the way his smile pulled back on one corner and the amused gleam in his eye. "You admitted you were bluffing," he pointed out.

"Not in the literal sense. But I'm glad everyone will take me seriously now that I broke open the mayor's murder investigation."

He smiled. "You're overconfident."

"And you haven't answered my question about Captain Webber."

"Why didn't you let Sergeant Hugo take down your information earlier?" he countered.

An answer I didn't like slid into my brain before my more conscious thought process could catch up. *I didn't need any more people to get close to in my life, and after two friendly dates, and a long, decent kiss goodnight, information like this might have made me feel closer to Hugo.* My chest tightened. "Is this a professional question or a personal one?" I asked, schooling my voice and features into neutral.

"Professional. Of course." He could do neutral well, too.

"How so?" I challenged.

"You could've told him, but you didn't seem to know you could. The department may have to do some work on showing we're trustworthy." He looked away. "Is that your car?" I blinked. The constant pivoting from one subject to the next probably made him a good interrogator, but it made me dizzy. I turned to see which car he was looking at. Pappa's old minivan was the only one in the visitor's section. For the first time, I noticed the license plate: I BURY U. "Uh, yes. That's my ride today."

"It suits you."

Instead of rising to his bait, I scanned the employee parking lot. There were seven civilian cars. "Is the black Ford Taurus yours?" I asked.

The glimmer of humor was back in his eyes. "Yes. Good guess."

"Hardly a guess. It's so you."

He lifted an eyebrow. "I chose it because it was nondescript."

"I gathered. You seem to have a thing for nondescript." I glanced at his blue tie and charcoal suit.

"Not always." Something in his voice made my gaze slide up. Our eyes met, and for a moment, I could swear the unflappable Brian Mahoney looked as confused as I suddenly felt.

I turned to walk to the minivan.

"About that speech you were anticipating," he began, falling into step beside me in one long stride. I wondered if, given enough motivation, I could outrun him.

His speech about not telling anyone what I had learned about Tilly Sandberg was to the point and patronizing in its clear attempt not to be. By the time he finished, I was sitting in the minivan, and he had one arm draped over the door, and the other braced against the roof. "Yes, sir, Lieutenant, sir. Now, can you tell me if you already knew Tilly Sandberg had a twin?" I asked, knowing he wouldn't tell me, but figuring it was worth a try.

He straightened. "There's a murderer out there, Angie, and the last thing I want is to be worrying about you, too. The questions you put to Tessa Baker might already have put you in danger."

I lowered my voice to an excited whisper. "*You think the murderer is Tessa Baker*?!"

"For the love of…" He looked heavenward for a good five seconds before fixing his gaze on me once more. It was the first time I'd seen him come anything close to exasperated. "Tessa Baker is a notorious gossip. Half the city probably knows you went to see her and why. If the murderer finds out, they could put a different spin on your questions, and rightly so. Did you think about that?"

I hadn't, but I thought about it now and was pleased to see it didn't bother me. Not one bit. My practical Gomez genes ran strong in the thinking-before-acting arena, I was sure, and I didn't think I had asked anything that would get me into trouble.

"Has anyone ever told you that you're easy to read?" he asked.

"Yes. All the time. Its why I stick to the truth." I smiled despite myself because sticking to the truth did not include omission in my book. The trick was knowing you were omitting for the greater good. That eliminated guilt and guilt was a strong emotion, and strong emotions are what usually gave me away. "And because I'm responsible and I don't want anything I do to affect your case, you should know that I spoke to Maddie Lentil, too, and my *extremely circumspect* questions only revealed that the current Tilly Sandberg didn't have a birthmark." He took a step back, ran a hand through his hair yet again, and opened his mouth for what could only be a scold I didn't have time for, so I preempted him by rattling off every word of my conversation with Maddie.

His face was a study in blankness again. Maybe I'd sculpt it one day and call it, *Unknowable.* "Sergeant Beemer should be done with an assignment by now, and she and I need to go over everything. Is there anything else you left out?"

Bonnie is dead. I did know more than I was letting on, and it was important. I looked up at him, struck by what I *had* to say. "Whoever killed Mayor Sandberg knew she was really Bonnie and confronted her about it."

"We haven't even established your theory is correct. How could you know that?" Hard eyes searched mine. "You can't withhold evidence, Angie."

"Call it a feeling. It's not anything you could put on a report or anything you could call obstruction." I smiled. "Don't worry."

He gave me a look. "Is the way you know this anything like the way your grandmother says she knows things?"

I crooked my finger and beckoned for him to come closer. The look on his face told me he didn't fully trust me, but he leaned down anyway. I whispered, "I hear dead people," in his ear, but I had a hard time stopping what my Abuela Luci called my unholy grin from spreading. There was something delicious about telling him the truth, knowing he'd never believe it.

He turned to look at me, his face inches from mine. "When you're in a playful mood, the little lights in your eyes dance. Did you know that?"

I felt light of breath, even though he didn't look like he was flirting. But why make an observation like that if he wasn't flirting? The answer that came to mind was that he was trying to throw me off balance again, to see if I revealed anything. I tilted my head and studied him right back. He gave his head a slight shake, straightened, and left without another word.

I was eager to go over everything with Pappa and Anthony, but when I got to the funeral home, they still weren't there. Exhaustion consumed me, and suddenly all I wanted to do was go home, cuddle with Tito, and sleep.

Detectives would have to tell Brenda that the dead body wasn't her actual mom as soon as they confirmed it. Mayor Sandberg had been loved while the old Tilly Sandberg, from twelve years ago, had been pretty much loathed all around. Would they want to celebrate the life of someone they had all come to care about, even if she had lied about who she was? Would Brenda even want to go through with the funeral?

And would Pappa and Anthony be angry with me that I hadn't shared my information with them, first? It had only been one day, but what they knew about me was monumental. It felt like we were a team. We were the only ones who knew *for sure* that that the murderer had known about Bonnie, that trying to deny it had been her last words. And that meant we weren't done with the case.

SIX

"Trying to still gossips' tongues is like putting up doors in open fields."

MIGUEL CERVANTES SAAVEDRA;
DON QUIXOTE

After my third cup of coffee, I went to my closet and grabbed the first funeral-home appropriate unwrinkled skirt I saw—a long, lightweight, black, and white Greek key-patterned wraparound. Normally I would pair this with a tank top or a V-neck T-shirt, but I felt my destination called for a black button-down shirt, even though another hot and humid day awaited.

I tried to walk Tito, but he became outraged when his nemesis, a designer Shih-Poo from down the street, peed in our front yard, right in front of his face. Tito then insisted on peeing in every corner of our yard until he was panting with dehydration, and then pulled me to the Shih-Poo's yard, where he pooped and peed.

Abuela Nydia had given Tito to me, and he was just like my mom's whole side of the family. "Calm until provoked. Indignation loud and never subtle," I said, shaking my head at him as I cleaned up his business. He looked into my eyes and barked twice, raising his head higher each time. "I know, I know. I get that from them, too. I'm not saying it's a bad thing." We went home, I poured Tito some water, and at fifteen to eight, I stepped out the door to see Abuela Luci had been about to knock.

Her eyes lit up the moment she saw me. "Oh, good, you're wearing the skirt I got you. The spirits screamed that it was you the moment we saw it, and now I see why. It's perfect for your new job. Somber colors, but with a creative flair, you know?"

"My new job?"

"Postmortem reconstructive specialist. I looked it up."

I paused, not quite ready to allow the idea to take root, but not ready to refute it, either. Carefully I said, "I think I did a good job, Abuela. Mayor Sandberg looks like the person we all knew, and she looks at peace."

Abuela gave me a look of disbelief. "But no one knew her, *nena*. She was an impostor."

My jaw dropped. "You know?"

"Everyone knows."

"*How*?"

Abuela sashayed over to the porch swing in her favorite red espadrilles, patted the seat beside her, and spilled the latest. Late last night, Brenda Mumford asked Pappa if she could come down to the funeral home to see how her mom had turned out. Lieutenant Mahoney and Sergeant Beemer arrived a short time later, to look over Mayor Sandberg once more, and they took the opportunity to question Brenda about a certain missing birthmark. They then showed Brenda records from a now-closed orphanage in upstate New York, stating that Tilly Sandberg was an identical twin. When they shared their belief that this twin had taken Tilly's place twelve years ago, Brenda became distraught. They couldn't reach Brenda's husband, so Brenda called Tessa Baker to take her home… which is, of course, how the entire city found out before midnight." Abuela shook her head. "It's just like one of those telenovelas we love. The long-lost evil twin trope. Only the real Tilly was the evil one in this case."

"*La Sombra de Alondra*," I said, remembering the telenovela where Alondra's shadow seemingly came to life at night and wreaked havoc on real Alondra's life, who was always sleeping while the wreaking took place. In the end, it turned out it was a hitherto unknown wicked twin sister who had been abandoned at birth because the mom had sensed evilness in her. My personal opinion was that being abandoned because your mom got weird vibes from you as a baby, and then finding out your twin sister was kept and loved, probably had a little something to do with the wickedness.

"*Aventurera*, *Marisol y la Luna*, and *Edmundo y Raymundo* all had evil twins in them, too," Abuela added.

"We should re-watch them," I suggested, thinking they might contain clues about evil twins. Real life was stranger than fiction, people said, so why not?

Abuela got up, and I walked her to her Kia Soul, making plans for a telenovela, food, and piña colada marathon along the way. She offered me a ride, but it was a beautiful day, and I thought a walk would do me good. Abuela peeled off, and a moment later, a white, windowless van pulled up beside me. The driver had a baseball cap pulled low over their head. "Hop in. I'll give you a lift."

"Ha!" I said, backing away and getting ready to run.

"Wait, it's me!" The driver popped their cap off, revealing the curly head, bright red lips, and pretty face of Nalissa Jones, a reporter for the *Dayton Gazette.* "And we need to talk."

Nalissa and I were not friendly. A few months back, she had published an opinion piece on how all psychic-related businesses were a sham, and she'd included every business in the region, including my grandma's. Abuela Luci had sent the article back to her along with a Nalissa-like voodoo doll. She didn't stick pins in it or anything—didn't want to be accused of issuing a threat—but noted that she had one just like it at home, and wasn't it adorable?

I put my hands on my hips. "First of all, I have a phone number even a bad reporter could find, since its plastered all over my website. Second, if you want to talk to a woman, you don't drive up to her in a windowless van wearing a baseball cap pulled low over your face."

"I thought you would recognize me, and I *did* try your phone."

Which reminded me I hadn't looked at my phone since last night. I took it out of my crocheted tote and saw it was blowing up. One deep breath and I dropped it right back in. "There is no way I'm granting you an interview about Mayor Sandberg," I said, knowing she probably wanted to interview anyone involved in any way. "I shouldn't even be seen talking to you because people will assume that's what I'm doing."

"No one can see inside the van—it's why I had the front windows tinted. And I have something that might persuade you to talk."

"The near-stranger with a vendetta against my grandma says she might have something that will persuade me to talk. Yeah, that'll work." I scoffed and began to walk away.

"That something is information about your parents, Angie."

A cold, painful prickle traveled down my spine. I stopped and turned. "My parents?"

"I have a lot of sources, and I did some digging."

I glared at her, trying hard to tamp down any eagerness. "Why did you brush off what I had to say last time we spoke?" Six months ago, I had asked her to investigate it. Instead, she'd written a hit piece on psychics, and then had the audacity to tell me I had inadvertently inspired the idea.

She sighed and ran a hand through her dark curls. "I want to start this partnership off on the right foot, so I will be brutally honest. I thought you were following up on theories you came up with as a hurt young girl, but that had no real merit. But I checked your story out anyway. And you can't hold my article on psychics against me because I know for a fact that it increased your grandmother's business tenfold—you can't deny it."

I couldn't deny it. Not about my grandmother's business benefiting, and not about being a hurt young girl desperate for theories. That was only a small part of it. Nonetheless, it was the part that made everyone, including my own family, not give my theory its due weight. "What do you mean by partnership?" I asked, aware now that she might be bluffing, the way I'd bluffed with Brian Mahoney.

"Get in. I'll tell you on the way to the funeral home. That's where you're going, right?"

"Yes," I said, and after a big, deep breath, I walked over to the passenger side.

"Shoot. Your grandmother just hit reverse," Nalissa exclaimed. I looked to see Abuela was two blocks down but zooming back in reverse, stopping only at the two stop signs to let others pass. She screeched to a stop next to me and narrowed her eyes at Nalissa. "I thought that was you." Before either of us could say anything, Abuela closed her eyes, shook her dark brown shoulder-length curls, put her palms up, and began to chant, "*¡Voy a hablar como una loca para asustar a esta desgraciada! Llámame más tarde y dime qué quiere esta cari-pelá atrevida contigo.*"

I nodded in agreement, and she waved and peeled away again.

"What did she say?" Nalissa asked as I opened the door and climbed onto the passenger seat. I couldn't tell if she was alarmed or amused. Probably both.

"She said, *I'm going to talk like a crazy woman to scare this disgrace of a woman! Call me later and tell me what this daring*... hmm... not sure there's a word for cari-pelá... maybe no-shame woman? Anyway, she told me to call her later and tell her what you wanted."

Nalissa laughed as she pulled onto the street. "I love your grandmother. It's too bad she'll never like me after that article. It would be fun to get an aura and Spanish card reading from her."

"I thought you didn't believe in any of that?"

"I don't. But I do believe some people have a knack for certain things, and your grandmother has a knack for reading people's character and needs. I also think her intentions and beliefs are genuine. She's not out to bilk anyone. I made that clear in the article."

"Your article increased her business, so she's not mad, she's just messing with you. The voodoo doll she has of you is now lying in rice, to bring you good fortune. I'm sure she'd be delighted to do a reading for you."

"Right. And mess with me some more."

"Only for the first few minutes." I thought about the doll lying in rice again. "*Have* you had good fortune lately?"

Nalissa smirked. "You don't really believe that one person can control another's destiny, do you? With rice?"

"Not with rice, but maybe some wills are stronger than others? It would explain a lot."

"I'd need evidence."

I smiled at that. "I had a bully in middle school who wouldn't leave me alone, and Abuela Luci promised me we'd take care of it together. I thought she was going to talk to the principal or the kid's mom, but she had another idea. When she couldn't find material around the house to make a voodoo doll of him and zip its mouth, she used a balloon to represent him instead. I drew his face on it, and she stuck a needle through his mouth and told it never to speak to me again, and he didn't."

She smiled. "You look like her, you know."

I nodded. I had my dad's big almond-shaped eyes, my mom's heart-shaped face and golden-brown hair, and Abuela's high cheekbones, too-full lips, and button nose.

But it was time to end the chitchat and get down to business. We were at a light, and the funeral home was coming up on the left. "So. You wanted to talk to me about my parents?" Anxiety pooled in the pit of my belly.

"Yes. I think there might be something to your theory on your dad's pendant being the target that night, and we can work on it together. But I need to know how you figured out that Tilly Sandberg's identity had been taken over by her twin sister twelve years ago."

I turned to gape at her. "How do you know I'm the one who figured it out?"

"It'll be all over the city soon."

"Yes. *How?*"

"Well, I went to Tessa Baker's this morning, since she was the one who began spreading the story, to question her. When she got to the part about how you went to her house last night to ask questions about Mayor Sandberg's hair, and who her past and present hairstylists were, we both realized you must have

Nalissa dove toward the back seat, rummaged through a bag and dug out a small notebook and pencil. "How did you find out about the birthmark?" she asked the moment she turned back to me.

"That's something only I would know. You can't credit an anonymous source."

"I can insinuate, without lying, that it was something you told detectives, because I do have a source at the sheriff's office, and most people have figured that out."

She knew what she was doing for sure. "Well, I *did* tell the detective I spoke to why I had gone to Tessa, and half the major crimes division should know by now." The urge to shake her until she told me what she knew about my parents threatened to overtake me then, and I took a moment to wrestle it down before turning in my seat to look at her. "Brenda told me about her mother's birthmark and how it couldn't be removed. It came up while we were talking about funeral preparations," I explained, deciding to leave out the detail about the picture. That way, I wouldn't have to describe the birthmark, the story would be vaguer, and I'd have plausible deniability of being a source. "Then, as I was preparing the mayor, I noticed there was no trace of a birthmark at all."

"Why did you go to Tessa, first?"

"To find out who Tilly Sandberg's hairstylist was, so I could ask her if she knew anything about an old birthmark. I thought maybe the mayor had managed to get it removed with some recently available technology, and I figured that's something her hairstylist might know."

Nalissa jotted something down and flipped the page. "What did you do next? Did you talk to Maddie Lentil? She won't pick up her phone, her voicemail is full, and her salon is closed."

Something nagged at me then, when she mentioned Maddie, but experience had taught me that whatever it was wouldn't come to me while my mind was occupied, so I set it on a back burner, so to speak. "Did Tessa already tell you everything I asked and everything she told me?" I asked, purposefully ignoring her question.

"In detail."

"Then you know that twelve years ago, Tilly switched from Lillian Carlson to Maddie Lentil, and like I told the detective I spoke to, it was the twelve-year mark that made me most suspicious of all. Everyone talks about how she had that near-death experience and came back a different person twelve years ago. She changed, she moved, and she switched hairstylists, even though Lillian Carson was now closer to her than before. I felt I had enough to go to the sheriff's office and not be laughed off."

Nalissa put her notebook down and eyed me speculatively. "People who were already wondering if the murder had anything to do with Neil Carlson's Woodruff building dispute are going to have a field day now that Lillian's name has come up, too. Not only did Lillian not need to do anybody's hair after she married Neil, but she couldn't stand Tilly Sandberg."

This was new. I sat up. "Do you know why? Is the person who told you reliable?"

She raised both eyebrows. "Are you asking me to name sources and methods?"

"If you tell me what you know, I'll let you know if I learn anything new that I feel I can pass on. It's not like I own a competing paper."

She shrugged and began to talk, and I realized this was what she had wanted all along. She'd played me, and if I was going to have any success in conducting my own investigation, I was going to have to learn to play, too. "Neil Carlson used Jessup Sandberg's commercial realty firm to find locations for his jewelry stores in Cincinnati, back before he got into real estate himself. Lillian's salon was in one of the buildings, and that's how she and Neil met. She was his tenant. And Tilly was Lillian's client, and she wasn't happy about their affair. She tried to talk him out of leaving his second wife to marry Lillian, but he wouldn't listen. He left his wife, Lillian closed her salon, and they got married, but as we now know, Lillian would drive up to Cincinnati to do Tilly's hair every six weeks and for special occasions. It doesn't add up."

"Maybe they reconciled?"

Nalissa shook her head. "I doubt it. Lillian badmouthed her all the time. Said she didn't buy Tilly Sandberg's good-girl act because she knew her too well from her days in Cincinnati. She still invited Tilly to all of her fundraisers because Tilly was the mayor and a popular one at that, but she and Lillian would only nod at each other once in greeting during the events." She pointed her chin at me. "Your turn again. Who did you talk to at the sheriff's office? Beemer?"

"You don't need to know that. What do you know about my parents' case?"

She studied me a moment. Every nerve in my body was strung tight. Finally, "The US Air Force Office of Special Investigations took over your parents' case years ago. The sheriff's office hasn't had anything to do with it since almost the beginning."

SEVEN

T*he US Air Force Office…*

It took me a moment to digest that, and when I did, pain forced out the air in my lungs. When I was finally able to breathe again, anger, so hot it burned my eyes, rushed through me. Why had the sheriff's office allowed me to believe they were investigating? Did this mean I was right? *"Why didn't anyone ever tell me?"* I choked out.

"It's par for the course, Angie." Her tone, which had been detached until then, gentled. Her eyes were kind.

My mind went back to the day I met with Brian Mahoney, and something he said toward the end came back to me. Cold case files still under our jurisdiction are a priority for me. *Still under our jurisdiction…* My parents' case was not.

Why the hell had he led me on? Why had he insisted I start at the beginning of my parents' story? My palms began to hurt, and I looked down to see I was clenching my fists so hard that my nails were digging into my palms.

It all seemed so utterly cruel that a grain of doubt filtered in. "How do you know this?"

"I have a source who worked in the department during that time," she said in a matter-of-fact tone, but I stored her exact words away, with the sense that she had also worded her statement carefully. "There's more, but I need to know if you'll work with me to find out more about your parents and the Tilly Sandberg case."

The smart reaction would be to think about it and get back to her later. But the need to know anything and everything about my parents was too great. "I'll work with you for as long as our goals align. My only goals are to find out who murdered my parents and why, and to see justice served."

Our eyes met. "I'm not sure how much you've been told, but a witness did come forward while the sheriff's department was still investigating your parents' case. A woman said she overheard your mom talking about a custom-made necklace she would be wearing the night of the reception, which gave the sheriff's department, and the Air Force Office of Special Investigations, a motive for the murder completely unrelated to the Air Force. They even neatly explained away your insistence that your father always wore a pendant around his neck and that it was the only thing missing. The perpetrators were after a unique-looking necklace your mom had been talking about, and according to you, they got one."

My heart sped up. I had opened countless boxes holding my parents' possessions since the day I'd spoken to Mahoney, but so far hadn't found my mom's agendas. And it had been difficult. Memories brought on nostalgia, which brought on deep, painful angst. "That's the only thing I've ever been told, and only recently at that," I said. "Do you know who the witness was?"

Nalissa shook her head as she watched me. "I don't. But I know how you can find out…" I waved my hand impatiently for her to get on with it. "The witness who supposedly overheard your mom talking about the necklace said it was at Lillian and Neil Carlson's tenth-anniversary party. She said it was during dinner. Lillian has a large collage of pictures from that night in her main living room. If you can get into her living room and find a picture of your parent's table, you'll narrow down who it could have been."

"Lillian Carlson," I repeated, surprised that her name was coming up yet again, and this time with my parents' case. My pulse began to race. "How do I get into her living room?"

She pulled out a folder. "They're hosting an event tonight for the LOWO fund. Tickets are one hundred dollars and sold out. I can get you in. I'll be there, too, as wait staff for the caterer, and I'll guide you."

"But you'll be recognized."

She leaned toward me, her eyes sparkling. "I'm a master of disguise, and because I know you have the skills to recognize me anywhere, I'll let you in on my secret. It starts by training people to only notice certain things about you in your everyday life. I keep my hair big and curly, slather on bright red lipstick every day, never wear heels, and always wear bold colors. People have learned to identify me by my hair, lips, height, and colorful clothes. The moment I throw on a wig, wear lifts or heels, put on a subtle lip color, and wear soft colors, I become someone else."

I studied her for a moment. She was petite, her features were perfectly symmetrical, her teeth straight and white, and her dark tan skin was smooth and free of blemishes. It all allowed her beautiful hair and crazy red lipstick to draw the eye, and you couldn't help but remember you had to look down to talk to her because of her short height. I was five foot four, and I probably had three inches on her. "Brilliant," I said.

"I know. Now back to business." She slid a picture out of the folder and handed it to me. "This is Ashleigh James. She's Lillian Carlson's best frenemy if you will. Do you know her? And, more importantly, does she know you?"

I studied the picture of the forty-something-year-old local socialite. "Yes. We've talked, but we're not friendly or anything."

"That's fine. Ashleigh will be drawn to you like a moth to a flame because of your role in uncovering Mayor Sandberg's true identity. She's going to secretly love that Lillian's name is being dragged into it, and she'll try to get more information out of you. But I need you to encourage her to gossip about Lillian and Tilly's relationship."

I looked up from the picture. "You want to know what made Lillian travel all the way to Cincinnati to do Tilly Sandberg's hair, regularly."

She nodded. "Everyone thinks that Tilly must've had something on Lillian, and Ashleigh will be the best source for old gossip and rumors. But you'll need to wear a mic and earpiece to communicate with me. I might catch something that you miss, and I can also guide you. The party's outdoors, and we'll need to seek an opportunity to get you inside to find those pictures of the Carlson's tenth anniversary."

"You're a more serious reporter than I gave you credit for," I said, careful to keep my eagerness in check. I still didn't know if I could trust her—if she was lying to me and using me simply to get information about Tilly Sandberg and Lillian's relationship.

The corner of her mouth lifted. "My dad has been a private detective for thirty-two years, and he's the best and most sought after in Southeast Ohio because he's skilled at reading people. I've worked with him and learned a lot." Her eyes caught mine. "I'm not interested in reporting on people who make mistakes. I'm interested in bringing down powerful evil-doers, Angie." Maybe she and I were more alike than it seemed on the surface…

My mind quieted its doubts and began planning. "I have a strappy gold dress I can wear to concoct a believable wardrobe malfunction. I can go inside to deal with my emergency, pretend to get lost, and look for the collage."

"Good thinking." She raised her hand for a high five, and while it didn't feel like a high-five relationship yet, I complied.

Nalissa then handed me her notebook and pencil. "Write your name down exactly as it appears on whatever government ID you'll use at the gate. I have to get it to my contact by this afternoon."

"I won't have a date, though. Will that look suspicious?"

She shook her head. "It's a huge event, with lots of support, and I'm sure plenty of people go solo." I handed her the notebook, and she read, "Angelica Gomez Gomez. Huh. Wouldn't it be easier if you just use one Go—"

My hand went up. "Don't."

After looking both ways and making sure no one was around, I hopped out of the van and made my way to the funeral home. It dawned on me that I hadn't asked what the LOWO foundation was, but I could always look it up. I dug my phone out to do a quick search but saw I had seventy-four texts and twelve voicemails. Eleven texts were from Anthony, two were from Pappa, and others were from local reporters, and friends and acquaintances—even people I hadn't heard from in years. The gist of it was that everyone now knew the details of my conversations with both Brenda Mumford and Tessa Baker last night, and everyone wanted an inside scoop. Eleven voicemails were from my Abuela Nydia in Puerto Rico. Somehow, it didn't surprise me that she'd found out. She had a google alert on my name. I listened to the one voicemail from a number I didn't know. It was another reporter.

Pappa's and Anthony's texts didn't tell me much about how they were feeling. Would they be upset that I hadn't told them about the missing birthmark? We had said we would share information, never guessing that I'd stumble onto information too huge to tell anyone but detectives.

But they were the only two people who knew I had heard Mayor Sandberg's last thought, and right now, with everything that was going on, I was glad two people knew my secret. They were the only ones who would be as certain as I was that Mayor Sandberg's murderer had confronted her about her true identity in her final moments. The sheriff's department, and even Nalissa, had to devote resources to investigating different leads if they come up. Anthony, Pappa, and I could focus solely on the Bonnie angle, and I could tell them about the gala.

I walked through the front door to see Anthony talking to Jim Russo. Anthony's eyes lit up when he saw me. That, at least, was a good sign. "Angie, this is Mr. Russo. Mr. Russo, this is Angie Gomez Gomez. She's our reconstruction specialist for the mayor."

"It's *Dr.* Russo," he corrected. "I recently received my doctorate. And good luck working with Miss Gomez. She doesn't accept constructive criticism."

Jim Russo had tried to tell me how to do my job back when I was doing initial sketches of the mayor. I felt about him the way Tito felt about the Shih-Poo from down the street. "I welcome feedback from people who understand my craft. Every professional I've ever worked under would agree."

He pursed his lips. "Well, I just saw the reconstruction work you did on the mayor, and she's smiling like the Mona Lisa. I don't think it's appropriate or professional, especially given the circumstances."

"Brenda Mumford was pleased with my work, and her opinion is the one that matters."

He shot me a superior smile, and I instantly saw where I had gone wrong. "Brenda Mumford is no longer the person who needs to be pleased. She isn't the mayor's daughter because the mayor wasn't the real Tilly Sandberg. And the prepaid funeral plan is void because it was made under Tilly

Sandberg's stolen identity. I've offered to step in and pay for the funeral. Your work will need to be redone, and your services will no longer be needed."

The implications for Pappa hadn't occurred to me until that moment. His business would suffer now that Mayor Sandberg had been revealed as an impostor. Who would want to pay their respects to her now? And if the prepaid plan were invalid, he'd lose money on top of losing the good publicity he'd been hoping for.

"We never accepted your offer," Anthony cut in. "And we're excited about Angie's work. We hope to partner with her again in the future."

"That's right," Pappa said, and I looked back to see him shuffle out of his office. "We're sorry we're unable to come to an agreement with you, but we stand by Angie." He turned to me. "Dr. Russo here said he'd do his duty and pay for the sinner's funeral, but at one fourth the price, and if we display a poster for his organization, House of Accountability, in each of our viewing rooms from now on. Anthony was about to decline and walk him out."

My heart then swelled. Anthony and Pappa had defended me, even though they risked alienating someone who could bail them out of the Mayor Sandberg mess. They wanted to work with me again. And the idea…

Was intriguing. A little lightbulb clicked on in a corner of my mind, but I couldn't pursue its light with Jim Russo's odious face glaring down at me. "Pride goeth before destruction, Angie Gomez! And a haughty spirit before a fall." He turned and made his way across the lobby.

I turned to Anthony and Pappa. "I'm so sorry, this is your place of business, and you were both professional in your rebukes, but I was not. He's just one of those people who burns up all my good intentions by always peeing all over other people's yards, like a smug and unevolved alpha dog who thinks all yards belong to him simply because he can lift his leg, and I had already kept my mouth shut and pretended to listen to him once when I was first working on Mayor Sandberg's bust, and I had a hard time forgiving myself for that, and I just couldn't do it again. I don't respect him because he doesn't respect anyone. Look at what he did to poor Pastor Johnson, took half his flock away—"

"Including Mayor Sandberg," Pappa mused, interrupting my rant.

Anthony gently took my hands and pulled them down. "Be careful with all that, um, gesturing," he said. "You're going to accidentally knock Pappa down."

"I've never knocked anyone down," I said, giving him a look. "And what was that about Mayor Sandberg?" I turned to Pappa again.

"Mayor Sandberg was one of the first people Jim Russo convinced to join his organization," Pappa explained. "He's controlling and a big fan of guilt and shame. He thinks making people feel bad about themselves gives him power over them, and he's convinced most people deserve hell on earth as penance for not being perfect." He paused, thinking for a moment, before throwing a subtle glance Anthony's way. "And being stuck in shame and guilt *is* a form of hell on earth."

I didn't want to intrude, so I looked away, but I was beginning to think of Anthony as a friend, and I wished I knew more about him. Was he living in his own sort of hell? Why was he no longer a criminal defense lawyer?

Pappa turned back to me. "My point is Mayor Sandberg must've been living with guilt and shame if she joined Russo's outfit. She might have even confessed to him. We're looking for people who knew about Bonnie, and it's possible he was one of them, don't you think?"

"Yes! You're right! But how can we find out for sure?"

Pappa's back suddenly went ramrod straight, and his eyes sparkled with the vitality of a man half his age. "I have an idea! Is Russo still outside?"

Anthony had the best view out of the front door. "Yes. He's sitting in his car, yelling into his phone."

"Get him! Tell him I decided to accept his offer." Anthony shrugged and jogged off. "Angie, come with me!" Pappa shuffled away faster than I'd ever seen anyone shuffle, and I followed him, excited because, for the first time, it felt like a real partnership. "Bonnie's name hasn't gotten out yet," Pappa explained on our way down to the embalming room. "Only detectives, Brenda, and the three of us know it. Jim already told me Brenda isn't answering his calls." He glanced back at me to see if I was keeping up. "Do you see where I'm going with this?"

"Um. No…"

With no time to lose, Pappa explained his plan.

It was bold.

It was risky.

And even with danger lurking, it was also fun. I needed some fun.

Soon I was outside, crouching atop a dumpster with my ear to the embalming room vent. Anthony was (hopefully) bringing Jim Russo down to meet with Pappa again.

"Your grandson here tells me you decided to accept my terms," Jim Russo's booming voice reached me.

"Not exactly," Pappa responded. "I came up with a counteroffer instead."

A short pause, and then, "Well, then, get on with it. I don't have all day."

"I propose you pay full price, and we don't display your posters."

Another pause in which I pictured him about to implode. "That is not a counteroffer! It's an insult, and you're wasting my time!"

His response was my cue. I turned to the vent, hoping there were no lingering formaldehyde fumes there, cupped my mouth, and howled, "Bonnie *is* dead!" I then quickly put my ear back to the vent. How I wished I could see his face! There hadn't been time to set up a recording device.

"Huh? What was that?" Jim Russo asked, sounding confused.

"It was a counteroffer," Pappa replied.

"No. Not that—the ghoulish voice…"

Anthony, who hadn't been in on the plan, had clearly caught on because he repeated, "Ghoulish voice? My grandfather's voice is a bit gravelly, but I'd hardly call it ghoulish."

"You didn't hear that?" Russo demanded. He sounded suspicious now, but his voice still held some doubt. "The voice? Saying something about a Bonnie being dead?"

"Oh. *The voice*," Pappa repeated in a knowing tone. "We hear the voice sometimes, too. But only if it wants us to hear it."

"You must be the chosen one this time," Anthony added, and it took all I had not to laugh. "What did the voice say?"

"I told you what it said! What's going on here?"

"Pappa wanted to make you a counter-offer."

"Stop it. I'm not playing your games. Where's Gomez?"

"Upstairs somewhere," Pappa answered. "Please leave her be. You've insulted her enough."

"You're all insulting me! I'm no fool!"

"Where are you going?" Anthony asked.

"Leaving!" Russo yelled, but his voice was closer to me now, directly under the vent. The man was smarter than he looked. He was leaving out the back door.

EIGHT

"The devil knows more for being old and experienced than for being the devil."

SPANISH PROVERB

I'd never make it up the driveway in time, and only in telenovelas could you get away with hiding behind the very door the villain was about to open. Panicked, I took in my surroundings. Rusted awning high above the back door. Dumpster I was crouching on. Dinky tree. All three?

I jumped from the dumpster to the tree, climbed up a few branches, and took a flying leap onto the rusted awning, feeling like a character out of The Matrix. A moment later, the door opened, and Jim Russo and Anthony walked out. "It's all right, Dr. Russo," Anthony said in soothing tones. "Some people aren't comfortable with the great beyond."

"I'm perfectly comfortable with the great beyond," Russo shot back. He took a quick step to the left to glance up the narrow side yard, and then took a few steps back and craned his head to get a good look up the long driveway to the right. He then stared at the dumpster under the vent with a knowing look. He walked over, lifted the lid, and frowned. Next, he looked up the tree, and then into the shrubs. He turned in a circle to take in all his surroundings.

"What are you doing?" Anthony asked.

"I'm sure you all think you're very funny! I'll walk myself to my car now. I don't need your escort." He started up the driveway, but then did a fake-out and practically ran back into the embalming room. He was going to rush up the stairs to look for me. It was ridiculous, but then big egos always resulted in ridiculous people.

I slid off the awning, where I'd watched the entire thing through a rust hole. Anthony caught me by my legs and carefully set me down before I took off. It was an uphill run, but I was motivated. Giving Russo and his ego the upper hand would eat my reasonably-sized ego alive.

I didn't stop running until I was sitting in Pappa's chair in front of his computer. I wiped the sweat from my brow, typed in a search term, and caught my reflection on the monitor in time to remove a leaf from my hair, just as Jim Russo came up the stairs that faced the office. It took all I had not to breathe heavily or take in great gulps of air.

I looked up.

"What are you doing?" he asked as he walked in and tried, but failed, not to pant.

"Looking up reports of ghosts in funeral homes. What are *you* doing? You look like you're going to have a heart attack."

He came around to look at the monitor. The screen showed images of apparitions. "Why?" He crossed his arms.

"Because I saw something float up the stairs a few minutes ago. Not that I expect you to believe me. Now please excuse me. I don't appreciate you looking over my shoulder like this."

He studied me carefully. I was not a runner. My throat was burning, I was holding the leaf in my fist, and I wanted to heave. I raised an eyebrow at him. He made an angry sound and finally left.

When I was sure he was gone, I walked over and opened the door to the basement. Anthony was waiting on the first step with a tall glass of water. I drank it in one gulp and followed him down. "The name Bonnie didn't mean anything to him," he said.

Pappa agreed. "But that was the most fun I've had in ages," he said and began to laugh, a big, deep, contagious belly laugh. Soon he and I were laughing so hard we were shaking and had to sit down, Pappa on a stool and me on the bottom step.

I waved my glass at Anthony, who had his arms crossed. He took the glass, filled it up again, and handed it back to me, saying, "Did it occur to either of you that if he *had* been the killer, he might have panicked and shot you for confronting him with his victim's last words? I would never have called him back if I had known that was your plan."

"Oh, I knew you had your Glock on you, and I trusted you to watch him closely," he said. "It was a smart plan." His eyes shone bright, and it made me happy to see him so animated.

"It was!" I came to his defense. "I didn't even need to see his face to know the name Bonnie meant nothing to him. It was in his voice."

Anthony took a deep breath before slowly letting it out. "Look, I'll admit I enjoyed yanking his chain, but only after I realized he wasn't the murderer. We can't just execute ideas willy-nilly like that. We're not trying to catch someone who stole lunch money here. We're talking about identifying a *murderer.* And people like Jim Russo, who are used to manipulating people, aren't easily manipulated."

"We know." Pappa sighed. "And we'll be more careful in the future, but I can't regret it. It was an unexpected light moment in what promises to be a difficult day." He turned to me. "Brenda asked me to give her until tomorrow to figure out what she's going to do about Bonnie. Her aunt, I suppose. Legally, the prepaid plan is void because she wasn't Tilly Sandberg. Detectives told us Bonnie was married but legally separated from a Roy Crawford, who doesn't want anything to do with her. It's a mess. Brenda has every right to wash her hands of the whole thing, which means I need to make other arrangements for the body."

"Oh, wow. It sounds like they already know everything about her."

Anthony heaved himself up on one of the metal tables. "They have the resources. All they needed was to know where to look, and you gave them that when you told them about the missing birthmark, and that Tilly had a twin." He looked impressed. "When did you figure out they were twins?"

I wondered if he thought I had figured it out immediately and had kept it from them. "The missing birthmark made a few things about the picture click," I explained before shooting Pappa an apologetic look. "I asked Anthony to text me the picture of the twins before you two left, since we had it already, and after studying it closely, I knew."

"Brilliant." Pappa smiled. "But we've been worried about you ever since last night when detectives came by to talk to Brenda and take another look at Tilly, or rather, Bonnie."

"I'm sorry. I didn't see your text messages until this morning, and then Abuela Luci came by, and then a reporter, and by the time I could answer you, I was already here. But I'm so glad you two aren't mad at me." It was… nice to be sitting here with them. I had enjoyed our camaraderie yesterday, too, beginning with the moment they had found a second body for me to listen to, to see if I really could hear dead people. And sharing a laugh with Pappa earlier had been good for my soul.

"Why would we be mad at you?" Pappa asked.

"For not calling you and telling you what I discovered before going to Tessa and then detectives, even though we agreed we were in this together."

He gave me a reassuring look. "You did the right thing. Time is of the essence in an investigation, and we're still learning how this partnership will work."

I looked at Anthony, to see how he felt about everything, but his mind appeared to be elsewhere. "*Bonnie is dead…*" He shook his head. "You heard it, and it helped uncover something huge. But there must be a scientific explanation for it all."

I smiled. "Abuela is sure there's a scientific explanation for all our relatives' gifts, but science hasn't caught up to us yet."

Anthony smiled too, which I now knew he didn't often do. "Someday, I'll ask you to list all their super-powers."

I thought of my Tía Carmen, who insisted angels spoke to her only while she did the dishes, and my Tío Roberto, who was best friends with two guilty ghosts who had repented but didn't think they deserved to be forgiven. One was a Spanish Conquistador, Sebastian, and the other was a Taíno warrior, Yaguax. "Enough that you know mine when not even Abuela Luci knows."

"You're not planning on telling her?" Anthony asked, eyes wide.

"I think she has an idea that I've come into a gift but would rather not know."

"What makes you think that?" Pappa asked.

I looked down at my hands. "Abuela came to live with us when I was still a baby. She left cousins, friends, and a successful business in the Bronx to be with us, but there was always this… a *sadness* behind her joy. I think she knew that my dad and mom weren't long for this world and that she had to squeeze the goodness out of every moment." I looked up. "And she did. But she also tried to keep them safe by interfering in decisions they made. She and my dad would argue about it, and I think she regrets that. If she knew my gift, she'd interfere, and I think she now senses she's not supposed to. She'll enjoy hearing all the things that came up just by working on the mayor and seeing that picture, though. She stopped by this morning, but we didn't have enough time to *chismear.*" They looked at me expectantly. "Gossip," I translated.

Pappa nodded, but Anthony frowned. "Wait—didn't you say a reporter stopped by, too? How would they know you were involved?"

I blinked when I realized I hadn't even told them about visiting Tessa Baker and Maddie Lentil last night to look for evidence to support my suspicions. I proceeded to fill them in on everything, beginning with my conversations with both Tessa and Maddie, and ending with how Nalissa and Tessa figured out I was the one who had gone to the police about the missing birthmark.

"Seems like everyone likes to *chismear,*" Pappa said on a sigh. "What else did Nalissa Jones want from you, then, if she had already figured it out? Confirmation?"

I hesitated then, not sure how much I wanted to tell them. But a moment later, I shook my head. I didn't trust Nalissa yet. I needed allies. "Yes. Confirmation. And… a partnership."

It was Pappa's turn to frown, while Anthony simply leaned in. "A partnership," he repeated with interest. His tone had warmed, and his hazel eyes had cleared. I noticed yesterday he did this whenever he sensed I was skittish and wanted me to trust him. It was mostly effective, except his left eyebrow's tiny movements gave him away if you knew to look. In truth, he was waiting for me to say something naïve.

Soon he'd be proven right. I was fine with that. Sometimes we had to set experience, wisdom, and judgment aside, and instead let hope lead the way. My dad told me once it was the secret to his greatest discoveries.

"You said you know what happened to my parents, but do you also know about my theory on the matter?" I asked.

Pappa didn't quite meet my eyes. "Yes. I've read and seen a few interviews you've given throughout the years. I filled Anthony in yesterday."

Anthony nodded. "Yes. The fountain of youth, gnat pupa, and the air force." His left eyebrow twitched.

I stood. "Well, Nalissa Jones has a source who confirmed to her that the US Air Force Office of Special Investigations took over my parents' case years ago. The sheriff's office hasn't had anything to do with it since almost the beginning."

Pappa's jaw dropped. Anthony directed a thoughtful look at the floor. Moments passed. Then, "I hate to say this, Angie, I really do, but what if she fed you exactly what you wanted to hear, to get you to talk about the mayor?" Anthony asked in careful tones.

Pappa looked pained but nodded his agreement. "Do you trust her?"

"I don't know, but…" How could I explain my gut feelings? "Look, I'm not an academic, like my mom was, or generally insightful, like my dad was, but I'm perceptive about the people and things I love and care about and am interested in. I watch and study and observe them, and I *know* my dad both feared and was excited about the pendant. I *know* he was protecting it. I *know* it meant something. And so yes, I believe Nalissa. But no, I don't trust her. That's why I need you." I began to pace as I filled them in on my visit to Lieutenant Mahoney the other day, the new information he had given me, and how it fit what Nalissa told me. I ended with her plan for me to go to the Gala tonight, and all my misgivings.

They were quiet for a long time. And then Pappa stood up. "I believe you, Angie, and I think I know a small way in which I can help, in case things go awry when you go looking for the picture of your mom."

Anthony's left eyebrow twitched heavenward, but when Pappa and I began to talk about potential pitfalls, he drew closer and threw in a few good suggestions of his own. "And what's this LOWO foundation?" he asked when we were satisfied with our little plan.

I took out my phone and went to the page I had bookmarked. "A knee and hip replacement fund for seniors who need but can't afford the surgeries, and it was named after Lou Owen Williams, an orthopedic surgeon, and philanthropist in the area."

Pappa stretched. "It sounds like something I may need to tap into soon…" An alarm on his phone interrupted whatever else he was about to say, and he stifled a sigh. "And that's a reminder that I have phone calls to make. I'll see you tonight," he said to me with a reassuring smile as he made his way to the stairs, but the spring was gone from his shuffling steps.

Anthony and I exchanged glances. Pressing business matters had aged Pappa before our eyes. It was sad, and I wished there was something I could do. "Should I work on the mayor's makeup? I didn't get a chance to finish last night."

Anthony nodded. "Bonnie Crawford may have stolen Tilly Sandberg's identity, but her wishes for her wake and funeral were her own, and Pappa's going to try to honor them where he can. Let's get her back on the table."

When we had her in place, I shone the light on her. "Her hair's all messed up."

"Brenda was showing detectives where the birthmark was supposed to be," he explained before going off to sit at the computer in the corner. "I'll be right here if you need me… trying to figure out the legal ramifications of this whole mess to make sure Pappa doesn't do anything that gets him into trouble…" He opened a folder, and then the laptop, and his voice trailed off.

I selected a comb from the tray and tried to recreate my efforts from last night, but the hairspray I had used was making it difficult. The curl on her chin was especially stubborn. I used my finger and more hairspray and leaned back to study my work. And that's when it came to me. The thing that had been nagging me about Maddie. "The inch!"

"Inch?" Anthony repeated distractedly.

"Yes!" I punctuated the air with the comb. "Maddie told me the mayor came into her salon every six weeks, like clockwork, to get half an inch off. But last night, I snipped a little over an inch off her hair to get it to look the way it always did. She couldn't have had her hair cut in at least three months!"

Anthony stood up and made his way over. "That's a good observation, but before you go accusing Maddie of murdering the mayor, let's think it through."

"I'm not accusing her of anything," I said through gritted teeth.

His hazel eyes twinkled for the first time since I'd met him. "The way you were slicing through the air with that comb spoke for you."

"Time is of the essence in an investigation, like Pappa said. We already eliminated Jim Russo as a suspect, and we now have a new clue. It can't hurt to ask her about it in a gentle and subtle way." I schooled my voice to show him how gentle my tone could be. "May I please borrow the minivan so I can pursue a clue, Anthony?"

"It *can* actually hurt. You don't know who the killer is, Angie and Nalissa Jones's article is already on the digital front page of the *Dayton Gazette*. It's the first thing I looked up when I sat at the computer. Your name is front and center, after Tilly's and Bonnie's."

My jaw dropped. "It's up already?" I hadn't looked at my phone in a while, and now I didn't want to. Hopefully, it had literally blown up.

He nodded. "She probably wrote it last night and was only waiting for your input to put the finishing touches on it." He shrugged then. "She's very good. She laid out the facts and timeline concisely, and no one would ever guess you were an actual source. In fact, she includes that you didn't respond to a request for comment. But Maddie might already know why you were poking around her salon yesterday. If she's innocent, it won't matter. But if by any chance she's not, then you have to be careful."

I looked up at him. "You know, you remind me of my other grandmother, Abuela Nydia. She curbs everyone's worst impulses."

"I'll take that to mean you agree with me." He grabbed the keys. "We can come up with a script on our way there."

Ten minutes later, we were parked in front of Maddie's, and we had a script. When I opened the door to her salon, she looked up from her client's hair and froze.

"Hi Maddie," I greeted her with a deferential tone that was meant to show her how sorry I was to bother her again. "I know you're busy, but could you spare me a quick moment?" I asked with an apologetic smile to her client.

"I'm sorry," she said to her client. "But I promise this won't take me more than a minute."

She walked toward us while pointing her scissors and mouthing, "*Out*!"

Anthony and I quickly backed out the door. She followed us. "You used me, and I don't appreciate it!" she hissed the moment the door closed behind her.

"Used you?" I repeated. So much for coming up with a script.

"Last night. You came around pretending to want to do right by Tilly Sandberg, or whoever she is, but you were fishing for information to take to the police."

"Because I couldn't just go around voicing crazy theories! I needed to be sure."

"Well, my name's in the paper now, and I don't appreciate it. You dragged me into it and gave me no warning." She turned to go, but Anthony stopped her with an authoritative, "Wait!"

Maddie turned back and gave him a withering look. "And who are you?"

"I work at the funeral home that hired Angie, and we noticed something else today that we hope you can clear up."

"Seriously?" She looked at us as if we were crazy. "You're not the police, Angie."

I folded my arms across my chest. "So, you'd rather I go to them and have them show up on your doorstep? How is that any better than being in the paper?"

She closed her eyes and pinched her nose. "Spit it out already then. What do you want to know?"

"You told me Mayor Sandberg came in every six weeks like clockwork, but last night I snipped a little over an inch off her hair to get it to look the way it always did. She couldn't have come in to see you for the past three months, but you also said she never missed an appointment." I rushed out.

"And where's your question?" she demanded. I couldn't understand why she was so upset with me.

"We're simply trying to figure out if it's important," Anthony said in soothing tones. "You say Angie didn't give you a heads-up last time, but now she is. If the mayor missed an appointment with you, and it was the very first time in twelve years, and you feel it was out of character, then maybe you should be the one to contact the police. It could help them figure out her state of mind in the days leading up to her murder."

She crossed her arms and gave us a disdainful look. "The mayor did miss her last appointment, but I completely forgot about it yesterday because I have a lot on my plate. Angie reminded me, and I told *actual law enforcement*, because it occurred to me, all on my own, that it might be relevant. So maybe stay in your lane and leave private citizens alone instead of accosting them in their place of business because you're bored and want to play detective." With that, she left.

My cheeks burned with mortification. I didn't need to be liked, but I also wasn't used to being disliked, and her attitude and tone stung. It wasn't like with Jim Russo, who I couldn't stand. I liked and respected Maddie. Or at least I had.

When we got back into the car, Anthony reached out to squeeze my hand. "I don't get why she's so mad at you, either. But she's right that we're playing at being detectives. You, Pappa and I know and understand why, but *you* need to understand you're going to make some enemies along the way."

"I don't care who hates me and who I have to take down when it comes to my parents. And I doubt I have anything else to contribute to the mayor's case."

"I'm not talking about your parents. Or the mayor."

"But I won't be looking into any other murders."

He tilted his head. "I'm not so sure about that, are you?"

NINE

"Get me out of this pickle, because it's already pretty messy in here!"

MIGUEL CERVANTES SAAVEDRA; DON QUIXOTE

I stood in the shadow of a palm tree near the infinity pool at the Carlson estate as people mingled and danced to a live jazz band on a beautifully landscaped patio surrounding the pool on three sides. "I feel like a third-rate spy," I murmured into my cleavage.

"Pull your shoulders back and tell yourself you're a clever woman who uncovered an important clue in a high-profile murder in our city and who will now use her fifteen minutes of fame and her resourcefulness to ferret out other clues." Nalissa's firm voice came in through my left earpiece. She was serving hors d'oeuvres and wearing a black and white catering uniform. Her transformation had floored

me. A long, straight, dark brown wig, pulled back in a low ponytail, hazel contact lenses, heels, and subtle makeup made her look like a completely different person.

She was also possessed of the amazing ability to talk without moving her lips. Earlier in the evening, she tried to teach me so I could be more inconspicuous, but my deep-rooted genetic tendency to use my hands to punctuate what I was saying kept giving me away. We'd decided to go with throat clearing and coughing codes if I needed to communicate.

"*Also tell yourself you look like a first-rate spy in that dress. Straight out of a James Bond movie,*" Anthony's voice came in through the earpiece in my right ear. Nalissa had not been happy about him joining us, but we insisted that his experience as a criminal defense attorney could help me formulate questions and get me out of sticky situations, should I land in one.

"*Isn't that just like a man to comment on her appearance,*" Nalissa mocked. I cleared my throat, hard—the code for *shut up*. They'd been at each other's throats since first sight.

After a few deep breaths, I scanned the scene from a purely tactical point of view. Lillian Carlson was holding court near the cash bar, and she didn't look like she'd be moving anytime soon. Neil Carlson was standing at the edge of a makeshift dance floor, chatting and laughing with a group of men. He was a big man with a round face, smug smile, double chin, awful comb-over, and the type of loud and self-important personality that attracted sycophants who believed that being obnoxious and having money made someone a leader.

But it was time to put my personal feelings aside for the greater good. I pulled my shoulders back, sashayed out, and owned the part of me that needed to see this through to the end. First, though, a piña colada. For the part.

Soon I made my way to Lillian Carlson's court. Those I didn't know kept chatting, but Lillian fixed hard eyes on me, and a silence fell over the crowd. Nalissa swore softly in my ear and said, "*I know that look. Prepare for bitch-off.*"

It hadn't occurred to me that Lillian would be upset with me. It should have, since Maddie was mad at me, too. But all I had been able to think about was getting inside the house to see who my mom had been sitting next to during dinner on the night of the Carlsons' tenth anniversary party.

My saving grace was that I often helped my older neighbors out with chores, and one of my favorite neighbors, Mrs. Goldstein, came up to hug me. I wouldn't have pegged her as part of Lillian's crowd, but she definitely needed a new hip. Perhaps she was there as a potential recipient of LOWO funds. "How wonderful of you to support our fund, Angie. I always tell people what a kind heart you have."

I smiled and thanked her, and then another woman turned from Lillian to me. Ashleigh James. Lillian's best frenemy. "Angie! How *brave* of you to come. *Everyone's* been talking about you. You'll be surrounded tonight!"

It was a provocative statement without appearing to be. "*Ignore whoever that was. Don't play her game,*" Anthony whispered. I almost nodded in agreement. The only way to get out of Lillian's line of fire now would be to kiss her butt but being a suck-up was neither a skill nor inclination I possessed.

It all felt like a classic telenovela. Or an eighties high school movie. The outsider in rich-people world. And that gave me an idea. "It's all pretty sensational, isn't it?" I looked at Lillian and widened my eyes as much as I could, which was a lot. "Everyone is so fascinated and wants to ask me questions, but all I did was notice there wasn't a birthmark on the woman's head. Were you as surprised as I was when it turned out the mayor was really an *impostor twin*?"

Everyone jumped in to start talking about it as if they'd been dying to bring it up but hadn't dared. As I suspected, Lillian became the center of attention for having known the original Tilly. No one here would dare imply she could have had anything to do with a crime and would instead feed her ego by peppering her with questions about what the real Tilly had been like.

Lillian reveled in the attention, and Ashleigh James' eyes lost their sparkle of mischief. I smiled an empty-headed smile at her and, in a low voice, remarked, "I was surprised when I heard Mrs. Carlson used to do Tilly Sandberg's hair. I always picture her doing only glamorous things, but I think it was so sweet of her to help an old friend."

"*Smart!*" Anthony whispered in my ear one moment. The next, Nalissa shushed him. "*Don't talk to her now unless it's absolutely necessary. She needs to focus.*" She was right, and I hoped Anthony wouldn't argue.

"Sweet of her?" Ashleigh repeated, without revealing what she thought of the word "sweet" to describe Lillian's action. She shrugged one shoulder. "It certainly was." She then treated me to a sincere look. "I mean if people were saying I was only doing my, uh… *friend's* hair because she was holding something over me, I'd stop just to prove everyone wrong. But Lillian must be a better person than I am because she didn't let what gossips were saying deter her." She smiled in Lillian's direction as if she were proud of her friend. And I looked at Ashleigh in admiration. Nalissa had been right about her.

"People used to imply that Tilly had something over Lillian?" I scrunched up my nose. "But that makes no sense. I mean, I've heard Tilly Sandberg, the real Tilly Sandberg, wasn't well-liked. If she had something big over another person, why would she simply make the person do her hair?"

Ashleigh James took a sip of her drink and sighed. "Exactly, my dear. It's why I never pay attention to rumors. Gilda Carlson, Neil's second wife, used to say Tilly did it to humiliate Lillian because she had been having an affair with Jessup Sandberg at the same time was having an affair with Neil…but you can hardly believe the scorned woman, can you? I mean, I always felt for Gilda, anyone with a heart would, but gossip is gossip, I guess." She was quiet for a moment and then hunched a shoulder before adding, "And the way the real Tilly used to call Lillian *honeytrap* could be interpreted as an inside joke, so maybe they were on good terms."

"Hmm. But I wonder how Lillian felt when the woman she thought was Tilly no longer wanted her to do her hair. It's all so complicated!" I took another sip of my drink and began to casually look around as if I were done with the conversation, and my comment was an afterthought.

For the first time, Ashleigh appeared thoughtful. "I mentioned it to Lillian a few times, but we both figured Tilly really had turned over a new leaf, what with her new zeal for public service."

"Ashleigh!" Lillian Carlson called, "I was telling Jeanne here about how the woman we thought was Tilly seemed to always avoid me, but I can't think of specific examples. Do you remember any?" Ashleigh walked off to join her.

"*See? You were clever and resourceful. That was great. I knew you could pull it off*," Nalissa commented.

"*You're using her, and she knows it. Don't patronize her*," came Anthony's voice.

"*We're using each other, and we both know it. What no one knows is what the hell you're really doing here*," Nalissa replied.

I cleared my throat again, put down my empty glass, and went to look for Mr. Carlson. If he was also upset with me for inadvertently bringing Lillian's name into the whole Tilly/Bonnie debacle, he needed to know Lillian and I were chummy, so I could have my wardrobe malfunction and enter the house without drawing his attention in a negative way.

Mr. Carlson and another beady-eyed middle-aged man were engaged in a serious-looking conversation, but their heads were turned toward the dance floor where they were both ogling a redhead with killer legs in a short, form-fitting sparkly blue dress. Interesting how they could multi-task.

"*I hate advising you on how to capture the weasel's attention for yourself*," Nalissa began, "*But get right in front of him, and he'll come to you. He's into curvier figures. His type always wants what they don't have at home. And you're alone. Which makes it more likely he'll approach you.*"

"*Don't let him get too close*," Anthony warned, sounding more like my cousin Javi than someone I had only met two days ago.

A moment later, someone put a new drink into my hand. I looked back, surprised to see Nalissa walking away. Three sips for courage later, I was on the edge of the dance floor, in their direct line of vision, my nearly naked back to them as Nalissa had instructed. I was swaying to the music and trying not to feel icky over trying to get their attention. Soon, Mr. Carlson and his buddy were on either side of me. My heart sank like a stone, even though it's what I needed to happen.

"Dancing is more fun with a partner," Mr. Carlson said, as his hand lightly touched my back. My skin crawled, and I had to fight the urge to shake him off. I turned to look at him. His eyebrows went up. "Miss Gomez," he said, without betraying thought or feeling.

"Miss Gomez?" The other man repeated his smile widening. "Aren't you the artist involved in the Tilly Sandberg case?"

"Yes." I smiled at him before turning to Mr. Carlson again. "Your wife and I were just chatting about the astonishing turn of events." Mr. Carlson followed my gaze to Lillian, whose expression, at once dramatic and amused, spoke of a woman enjoying the attention of the rivetted crowd around her.

Mr. Carlson's eyes smiled down at me. "Thank you for hosting this event," I said, to keep myself from cringing. "This is the first year I've been able to make time to honor a man whose generosity has helped so many."

The particular way Mr. Carlson paused told me that heightened awareness and suspicion were a part of his nature. A slight chill went down my spine as I wondered what I had gotten wrong, but I kept my gaze steady and warm. "What man's generosity?" Neil Carlson asked, his smile widening.

"*Anthony…what generous man is Angie talking about?*" Nalissa asked.

"*Lou Owens, the orthopedist who—*

Anthony's voice became an indistinguishable buzz in my ear when a familiar voice and another hand on my back filled my senses. "The law officer who rescued Angie's dad from a car wreck down in St. Augustine fifteen years ago." Brian Mahoney pressed his thumb on my back at the words *law officer*. To my annoyance, goosebumps erupted. "He took care of her dad until her family could fly there from Puerto Rico, and they found out he was just as generous with others as he'd been with Mr. Gomez. Sadly, the officer died in a boating accident six months later, leaving behind a widow and an orphan, and he's all Angie's been able to think about ever since I asked her to be my date tonight." This time he pressed down gently on my skin at the words *widow* and *orphan,* and I knew he was trying to send me a message… but I was stuck on the word *date*.

When Anthony yelled, "*All right, she's got it! But you should've told her from the get-go instead of giving her a damn abbreviation!*" in my ear, I realized Nalissa had been repeating the words *"Law Officers' Widows and Orphans Fund,"* to me, over and over again. I cleared my throat. It was thoroughly disconcerting to hear them arguing with Mahoney standing so close to me.

The corners of Brian's mouth laughed at me, even when the look in his eyes told me he was suspicious. "You're late," he said.

"Don't let him scold you, he's been plenty entertained," Carlson intervened, shooting an amused glance Brian's way. "But you can get back at him by dancing with me while he fetches the young lady who's been waiting for him over there some refreshment."

I turned to where Carlson was looking and saw the long-legged redhead in the sparkly blue dress was Joanna Danes, the administrative assistant at the coroner's office. The day we met came back in a flash, and I remembered Joanna had told Brian she'd see him on Friday. Well, it was Friday. Was she really his date? It made no sense that he'd claim me as his date when he already had one. Joanna waved at me, and I waved back, with as big a smile as I could muster, to show Neil Carlson all was well.

But as easygoing as Brian appeared to be, he apparently wasn't about to let another man steal his fake date. "I'll cut in as soon as I'm done helping you with your hosting duties," he said to Neil. It would be nearly impossible for anyone to take offense at his good-natured jibe, not with Brian's easy charm, but I knew it was also meant as another hint for me. Brian had something to do with organizing the fundraiser. Something I should know, seeing as I was his "date."

"Gross. I really hate this part on your behalf. Don't let him hold you too close," came Nalissa's voice.

"Don't fall for it, Angie. You're merely a source," Anthony said. *"A means to an end."*

"Jeez! Where does your animosity toward reporters come from?"

They began to argue. "I love the band," I said to Mr. Carlson, desperate for them to shut up. "The last party I attended had an orchestra that was so *grating*, it gave me a *pounding headache,* and I could *barely hear myself think*. I almost gave up and left."

Nalissa and Anthony shut up.

Neil Carlson's green eyes held mine as he gently placed my left hand on his shoulder, took my right one in his, and pulled me close. Clearly, I hadn't thought through every detail of the night. The way he was looking directly at me and the possessive way he was holding me seemed straight out of the overconfident playboy's guide to seduction. I couldn't ask his permission to enter the house when I suffered my wardrobe malfunction because he would no doubt take it as an invitation to help me with it, even though his wife was across the pool.

"This fundraiser means a lot to Brian," I began, smiling fondly when I said his name. "And to everyone in the law enforcement community. It's so good of you and your wife to host it every year."

Carlson smiled. "I was under the impression that Brian had tried to get out of being on the setup committee. Sheriff Whitaker had a hard time convincing him."

I shrugged a little. "That's Brian. If he doesn't think he can throw his whole heart into something that deserves it, he'll say so. In fact, I don't think Sheriff Whitaker was right to throw this at him. Brian is just getting settled into his new job, and the responsibilities are huge."

"It must get lonely for you."

"I have plenty of friends." I took a step away.

"Don't be jittery," Carlson said. He looked utterly amused. "I only want to be friends, too."

"Trust me, you don't," Brian said as he came up beside us. I don't know how he did it, but he managed to slip me out of

Carlson's arms and into his own as if Carlson and I had allowed it. "She's like a tick. Impossible to dislodge once she gets her teeth into you, and all sorts of trouble."

Carlson lifted an eyebrow at me, and I smiled and shrugged as if to say it was true. He laughed and walked away.

Then I scowled. "You show up everywhere, even in my soup."

He raised an eyebrow. "Your soup."

"It's a Puerto Rican expression for when you can't seem to get rid of a person. You look down, and there they are, even floating around in your soup." I pretended to sigh.

That got a half-smile. "A tick is still worse. It bites."

"So, what you're saying is, you're scared of me while I'm just tired of you?"

"Yes." His bright blue eyes searched mine. "What are you doing here?"

"What are *you* doing here?" I threw back, even though it wasn't clear to me where I was going with that. Here he was, throwing a wrench in my plans when everything had been going well enough. His eyebrow went up, just a smidge, but with enough of a challenge to get me back onto my game. "Seriously." I widened my eyes at him. "Why are you *here*, claiming to be my date and dancing with me, when your real date is over there?" I looked for Joanna Danes but couldn't find her. "Somewhere."

He hunched a shoulder. "I take my responsibilities seriously. That includes selling tickets to responsible citizens who won't cause trouble and rescuing crashers who don't even know been the one to figure it all out. She was thrilled to have been a part of it. The moment I left, she was on her phone, talking to Karen Schultz." She looked into my eyes. "I'm going to include your involvement in the article, Angie. You're already part of the story."

It annoyed me that the first thought to cross my mind was that Brian Mahoney would now be able to say he told me so. And that Abuela would have a *bioco* because I didn't tell her the whole story was the second.

Brenda Mumford was my last thought. Would she feel I betrayed her? It would have been wrong to tell her anything before I told detectives, and I hoped she understood that.

But, why would Brenda call Tessa Baker, a kind person, but a known gossiper, to pick her up, and to confide in? I shook my head. Again, it pointed to Brenda wanting people to find out. Had she known all along, as I'd suggested to Mahoney? "Look, I'm sorry, Nalissa, but I can't talk to you about this. This is all pretty huge, and people were mourning and in grief enough as it was."

"Remember that I'm not asking something for nothing. I'm offering a trade," she said as she pulled into an available parking spot near the funeral home. "So how about I ask you a few questions, you answer what you feel you can, and I credit you as an anonymous source with intimate knowledge of the investigation? You have to understand that when reporters responsibly amplify a story, it jogs more people's memories, and it often helps uncover clues."

I blew out a breath of resignation. She was right. "Fire away, and we'll see."

what the event is about. It's important everyone has a good time."

"I'm not crashing. My name is on the list."

"It wasn't on the list last night."

"I didn't get my ticket until today."

"Tickets were sold out two days ago."

"I didn't say I bought it."

"No. You did not. Who is Lou Owens, anyway?"

"An orthopedic surgeon who set up a fund for patients who can't afford hip replacement surgery. He replaced my dad's hip after that unfortunate car wreck you were talking about, and we became fond of him," I lied, to remind him how easily and smoothly *he* had lied. In fact, he had lied to me twice. I stiffened, remembering my anger at him.

Brian held my defiant gaze. "What am I going to do with you?"

"Stop lying, for one."

He didn't even blink. "What is Nalissa Jones doing carrying a tray of champagne?" he asked instead.

"How the hell did he recognize me?" Nalissa's voice hissed into my ear. "*That never happens.*"

"Nalissa who?" I wrinkled my nose and looked up at him.

His expression was serious. "Why are you wearing an earpiece?"

"*You shouldn't have let him close enough to see,*" Nalissa scolded.

"I didn't," I said to Nalissa before catching myself and saying, "...think anyone would notice. I'm hard of hearing." Selective hearing my Abuela Nydia called it.

He pulled me closer. "Oh, that I know. But you were also talking to your cleavage a little while ago. Then I saw a waitress hand you a drink you didn't ask for, and I began watching her. It took me a while, but I finally figured out who she was. Is she the person you're talking to?"

"Yes. She wanted feedback on her waitressing performance."

"Is she an actress now?"

"Good investigative reporters go undercover sometimes, and they need to practice."

"Thanks for confirming my suspicions. What is she investigating, and why are you helping her?"

Our eyes met, and I jutted my chin out. It was a good time to tell him that I owed him no explanations and that I would never trust him enough to tell him anything ever again. But the last thing I needed was Brian Mahoney following me around all evening. I finally had a clue about my parents' case, and I was determined to get into the Carlson home and look at the collage of the couple's tenth anniversary party to see who had been sitting next to my mother. Somehow, I had to get him off my back.

I pretended to fix my earing so I could dislodge the earpiece he'd seen because that one was Anthony's and not Nalissa's, but he didn't know I was wearing two. "Nalissa, can you pass close behind me?" I requested. Moments later, I sensed her behind me, and I discreetly gave her the earpiece. "There. It's gone. She and I can no longer communicate," I lied. "Does that ease your overly suspicious mind?" I looked into his eyes for a long moment. He was still close enough that I could feel his heat, his heartbeat, and his watch.

An idea lit up my brain, and I was unable to help the resulting grin. I'd use him. No one would suspect Brian. I slid my hand down to where his was at my waist, tugged at one of two strings I had rigged to malfunction, and slid my thumb across his wrist, caressing it. "Or do you want to handcuff me to you all night?" I asked, leaning in close enough for my breath to tickle his lips. Before he could answer, I wound the string I had carefully removed from my dress around the crown of his watch. "Oops. My dress got caught on your watch. It looks like you'll have to escort me into the house to fix it. We'll let Lillian Carlson know."

His eyes, which had gone wide at my flirting, cleared. "You must really trust me to leave yourself at my mercy like this. One little tug and…" He pulled his watch away, just a little, but enough to make me panic.

My free hand flew up to discreetly grab a chunk of hair at his nape. "Do it, and you'll be needing a toupee."

He smiled. "I think your hands will be too busy pulling your pretty dress *up* to try to pull my hair *out*."

"You wouldn't."

"You'd deserve it. But then I won't find out what you're up to." He readjusted his hand on my back in a way that gave him control and reminded me I was indeed at his mercy.

Brian steered me to Mrs. Carlson, who paused the moment she saw him, her eyes sparkling and flirtatious. But before he could open his mouth, I said, "Mrs. Carlson, Lieutenant Mahoney would like to know if you'll dance with him while I go inside to fix my dress." I turned us both slightly, to show her my back. A few people laughed, but I didn't have time to feel embarrassed. "His watch got caught while we were dancing, and I'm afraid of a wardrobe malfunction. Luckily, one of your waitresses saw it all and told me she has a needle in her bag. Oh, there she is."

Nalissa came up behind us and quickly but carefully freed Brian's watch. "There. I'll hold it in place while we go inside." She looked up. "I've waitressed here many times, Mrs. Carlson, and I know my way around. Is it alright if I take her to the powder room the catering staff uses?" she asked in a respectful and deferential tone that sounded nothing like her.

"Yes, of course. You'll have privacy there."

I turned to Brian, about to offer him a triumphant smile, when I realized I was counting on him to remain quiet. One word from him about me being up to something, and I'd be escorted off the estate. But somehow, I knew he wouldn't do that. Why? Why did I trust him when he had lied to me? It made me feel like I'd lost this round, even though he was leading Mrs. Carlson to the dance floor and allowing me to walk away.

"Anthony says you're banking a little too much on that dress," Nalissa said with a chuckle. I'd forgotten that Nalissa could still communicate with Anthony. We made our way up to the house in silence, and Nalissa made quick work of fixing my dress. "To the living room," I said, and we snuck our way to the other side of the first floor, careful not to run into anyone.

Nalissa pushed open a French door, we slipped into the room, and she closed it again. Enough light streamed in from an open window to allow us a good look at every photograph, while plenty of shadows kept us from being too visible to anyone on the outside. It was a large room, and we began our search in opposite corners. "I found them," Nalissa soon said.

"Are you sure?" My heart began to pound, and I turned to see her taking pictures of framed photographs on a table against the front wall.

"The invitation is framed, and it says, 'In Celebration of our Tenth Anniversary' and there are a few collages on the wall, and individual photographs on the table. Your mom must be in one of them. We'll check my pictures later," she said as she quickly clicked away.

The French door creaked open before I could reach her. "Hello, Lieutenant Mahoney!" Nalissa smiled brightly as if the two of them were running into each other at a coffee shop.

"Leave, now, through that side window, and I'll meet you out by the front gate," Brian said to her. "Mr. Carlson is on his way here with two friends. Angie, you leave with me."

"Aren't you supposed to be dancing with Mrs. Carlson?" I asked, exasperated by him.

"The dance ended a few minutes ago."

I had no idea we'd been gone that long. But Nalissa still had pictures to take. We were too close to give up now. I glanced around for a distraction and latched onto a picture of a car on the wall next to me. "I took a wrong turn, but when I saw this old picture of Mr. Carlson and a Porsche RS60, I couldn't help but get closer—do you think it was one of the originals?" Brian turned his wary gaze my way. "My dad used to love this car," I explained.

The sound of nearby laughter reached us. Brian turned to Nalissa, who was done and already climbing out of the window he'd pointed to. I hoped the last pictures wouldn't be too blurry. He then took my hand, and together we rushed to the door, but the footsteps and chatter were too close for us to escape into the foyer. Our eyes met.

"You're my date," he said as if reminding himself of his earlier lie. His eyes were on my lips, and he lifted his hand to cup my face. "If you have a better idea, say it now." My thoughts raced and got nowhere fast. I shook my head.

He bent his head, and it suddenly occurred to me that we could say he was helping me fix my dress because the waitress got called away. My mouth parted, but the words died the moment our breaths mingled. The sensation sparked a kind of hunger I'd never felt, and it drew me in as if I had no choice but to touch my lips to his. His lips touched mine for a moment that filled me to the brim with a mix of feelings, both emotional and physical, that I didn't quite understand.

We simultaneously breathed out, slowly, and I wondered if he too was struggling to keep himself in check. It was barely a kiss, and yet it felt like a tsunami had rolled over me. He lifted his head and touched his forehead to mine, and our eyes met for the space of a second before he wrapped his arms around my waist, and I pressed myself up against him, my hands on either side of his face, to make sure his mouth was at the angle I needed it to be when it sunk into my mine.

The initial reason for the kiss floated away, but it snapped back into my brain the moment I heard the "Ahem." A mortified glance revealed three men at the French door, amused looks on two of the faces, and a lecherous look on Carlson's. It took everything I had left of my wits to get my breathing, heartbeat, and embarrassment all under control.

Brian drew my hand into his and stepped in front of me. "Sorry, Neil. The waitress got called away, and the wait staff area was full. I came in to help Angie fix her dress in privacy, and I got carried away." His tone was one of calm, apologetic acknowledgment of the awkward situation, but his stance was protective. He was trying to shield me from the men's watchful eyes and warning them away from me, lest they get ideas. It made me feel breathless and funny… and a little offended. I didn't care what three slimy men thought, and I could protect myself!

"No need to apologize here. It's nice to see a young couple in love," Neil said. "How long have you two been together?"

"Angie and I have an on again off again thing," Brian answered. "I guess this means we're on?" he asked, gazing down at me. The look in his eyes told me the "on" meant he expected me to tell him what I had been up to.

"Oh. See, I thought we were off." I gave him an earnest look. "You don't open up to me the way I need you to, and then you get all upset when I act totally independent of you."

"There's a whole lot I want to talk to you about, but I doubt you want an audience." He lifted an eyebrow as if to ask, *or do you*?

"I never do. So, if you'll excuse us," I said with a smile before stepping in front of Brian, who was still holding my hand, to lead him out of the library. The idea of Mr. Carlson's eyes on my backside made me want to heave, so I kept Brian close behind me. The way he held my hand in his told me he had the same idea. My mind was searching for something biting to say as we made our way across the foyer and down the hall, but a deep, menacing male voice came through my earpiece, saying, "*Stop right there and put your hands over your head,*" and stopped me cold.

"Nalissa! Who is that?" I dropped Brian's hand and took off on a run but teetered every other step in my heels. Alarmed at my words, Brian followed me. "Where is she?" he asked.

"*Front gate*!" Nalissa answered.

"Front gate!" I repeated, and Brian quickly overtook me. To Nalissa, I said, "Tell Anthony! We have a getaway car ready!" It was supposed to be for me because we weren't sure we could trust Nalissa, but she needed it.

"*Anthony, I need a getaway car! I can't outrun him!*" Nalissa's panting words made me kick off my heels to catch up to Brian.

A moment later, dead silence. "Did you make it?" I asked. Nothing. No panting, no breathing, no words. I caught up to Brian on the driveway, we passed the front gate, and finally made it to the street where we saw a man looking into parked cars. "Hugo!" Brian called.

Sergeant Derrick Hugo waved Brian over, and we jogged up to him, while I looked around wildly.

"Angie." He nodded to me in greeting before turning to Brian. "I saw a woman hiding in the pine trees by the house. She ran when she saw me and kept running even though I ordered her to stop. The moment I turned to the street she was gone."

"Did you see anyone else around?" Brian asked.

Derrick shook his head. "Only Pappa from River's Bend Funeral Home in his hearse. He had just picked up a body."

I pressed my lips together to keep from laughing, and Brian's worried expression morphed into quiet understanding. "Did you happen to get a peek at the body?"

"I saw the body bag, why would I—" he paused. "You don't think—" He gave his head a quick shake. "It was Pappa," he said, as if there was no way whatever was in the body bag was anything other than a dead body.

Brian slowly shook his head at me. Words were not needed. I was being accused of corrupting Pappa. I turned to Derrick. "Are you working security?" I asked, noting his uniform.

"Yes, and I had better get back. You sure look nice, though," he said with a friendly smile. He told Brian he'd see him at the station and jogged off.

A honk made me jump a little, then, and I turned to see Anthony waiting further down the street in the minivan. My car was nearby, but Anthony was offering me an escape. "Well, there's my ride," I said to Brian, but he stopped me before I could walk away. "I think I know what you and Nalissa were up to. All I have to do is to check what she was taking pictures of to confirm, but why don't you tell me instead? So we can talk about it."

It hit me hard then that this man, and the sheriff's department, had been stringing me along with promises of cold cases being a priority for years. The level of disappointment in him that I felt made no sense because I barely knew him. I clenched my hands into fists. "If you suspect what we were up to, it means you now know that I now know more about my parents' case than anyone in the department ever cared to share."

My eyes felt wet, and I damned my overactive tear ducts. But I remembered that my mom always said that to allow oneself to be vulnerable in front of others was brave because it meant you weren't afraid of emotional pain. I looked up, not bothering to wipe away the tears. Let him see that I was hurt, but that I didn't fear it, and it wouldn't break my resolve. "You could have told me it was no longer in the department's hands. Anyone could have told me at least that much. But you're worse than any of the others. *You* chose to play with words *and* my feelings."

He ran a hand through his hair. "I chose my words carefully because I didn't want to lie to you, and I listened to you and asked questions because I do want to help. But I'm also trying to keep you safe. I wish you could trust that."

That blew my fuse. "Why? Why should I trust you, Lieutenant Mahoney? For heaven's sake, I spoke to you for the first time less than a week ago! And I don't need you or anyone to keep me safe! Or keep me anything!"

He took a step toward me. "Well, you sure as hell shouldn't trust Anthony Pappalardo, and it seems you do. Did you know Anthony before you took on Mayor Sandberg? Have you asked him why he was fired up in Cleveland?"

I lifted my chin. "I trust my instincts."

"And your instincts tell you not to trust me? And to keep digging on your own, even when you're hurting people who have nothing to do with anything. Like Maddie Lentil?"

"Maddie Lentil?" I repeated.

"You should've come to us the moment you suspected Tilly Sandberg was an impostor. But you began asking questions instead, and you brought Maddie Lentil's name into it. She's in the middle of an ugly custody battle, her ex's lawyer is a pit bull, and the last thing she needs is her name in the paper in relation to anything negative like that."

For the first time, I understood what Anthony had said about consequences and making enemies. He knew because he had been a criminal defense attorney, one who had apparently been fired. But I was new to all of this.

I understood now why Maddie was angry. And I had to figure out what I could have done differently. But I also knew what Mahoney was up to. "You're doing it again. Playing with my feelings, trying to make me feel like a bumbling idiot who goes around hurting people. Well, it won't work, because I know things you'll never know that will allow me to make a difference." I didn't care that I had said too much. He'd never figure it out.

I walked away, and when I got to the car, I turned to Anthony and asked, "Why were you fired?" because I needed to know. Suddenly, there were all these new people in my life, and I didn't know if I could trust any of them.

He studied me a moment before gripping the wheel and saying, "My ex was a prosecutor I knew was withholding evidence that could help save a young man from life in prison. I broke into their office at night and got caught. I might get disbarred. A hearing's coming up."

I breathed in and out a few times as I let the astonishing revelation sink in. "Did the young man get justice?" I finally asked.

"What I did saved his life, and I will never regret that. But if I had been more careful, more thoughtful, I might have found another way. Maybe I wouldn't have thrown away the education my grandfather worked hard to help pay for, and all those years of hard work. And I'd still be helping people."

I didn't know what to say, so I reached out and squeezed his hand, my heart heavy for him.

He dropped me off at my car, and I thought about his words for a long time.

TEN

"God save me from still waters! I'll save myself from the turbulent ones."

ABUELA NYDIA'S ENGLISH TRANSLATION OF AN OLD SPANISH PROVERB

I glanced at my watch, closed my eyes, and tried hard not to growl.

It was now officially a full twenty-four hours since Pappa had dropped Nalissa off at her car, and I still hadn't heard from her.

I wanted those pictures.

I felt like an idiot for trusting her.

I was mad.

On top of that, Pappa still didn't know if Brenda Mumford would go ahead with the memorial or funeral, and I was worried about his business.

"Okay. Out with it. *Que te pasa*?" Abuela Luci hit pause on *La Sombra de Alondra* and turned to me. Tito barked in protest. There were only two things he liked to watch on TV, telenovelas, and Dateline. We were in Abuela's living room, sitting on her comfy recliners, eating tostones with mayo-ketchup, and re-watching a telenovela I now remembered freaked me out as a child.

"Nothing," I answered. "Just trying to remember how Alondra's twin found her in the first place." I had already told Abuela about how Nalissa Jones and I partnered up so I could question Ashleigh James at the gala, and Abuela enjoyed the story, especially the body bag getaway part, but she didn't know we had also partnered up to find out more about my parents.

"Well. Alondra's aunt found a picture of them in the attic from when they were born and then went looking for the lost twin, so they could destroy Alondra together. They were accomplices." She turned back to the TV, hit play, and we watched Alondra once again be falsely accused by her fiancée of cheating on him with another man. I wished it was a villain slapping scene instead. I needed to hear a good slap. I stifled another growl.

"Ok." Abuela slapped her thighs and got up. "I didn't want to say anything, but your aura is looking ugly tonight. What's wrong?"

"Shoot! Is it *mucousy* again?" Last time she said my aura was ugly, I came down with the flu. Abuela knew before the first cough because my aura had been *mucousy*, as she put it.

"It's not *emotionally* healthy, I meant." She squinted at me while outlining strange shapes around my body. It's all bulgy and distorted but glowing with the fiery oranges and muted blues of a woman who feels betrayed and foolish." Her light brown eyes cleared. "Last time I saw something like this was when my Abuelo Enrique offered a ride home to my Abuela Celina's arch-nemesis, her cousin Francisca. Abuela Celina was so mad, she chopped up every one of Abuelo's cigars with a machete."

I sighed dramatically. "Well, it's nothing like that." Although chopping something up with a machete sounded liberating.

"Really? You don't feel angry and betrayed over something you don't truly understand? Because it turns out that it had been raining, and Abuelo Enrique had accidentally sprayed Francisca with mud while driving past her in his new jeep. He couldn't in good conscience leave her on the side of the road like that. Good thing, too, because she was about to cast some seriously bad vibes his way."

"Do you have a machete?" I asked.

"Yes. It's under my bed."

I wrinkled my nose. "Why under your bed?"

"In case there's an intruder at night. Some people keep a baseball bat under their bed, I keep a machete. It's scarier than a baseball bat, and I know how to wield it."

"Can I borrow it if I ever want to chop something up like Abuela Celina?" I asked.

"You don't have one?"

"No."

"Huh. We need to get you one, so you can keep it under your bed."

"Sounds like a plan." My phone rang then, and I dove for it. The caller id said it was Pappa. "Hello?"

"Angie?" His voice was hopeful.

"Yes."

"I know it's late, but would you mind coming down here? Brenda Mumford has decided to move forward with a private service and funeral. Only she'd like to talk to you about making some changes to Tilly, er, Bonnie Crawford, first."

Eager to do something other than wait for Nalissa Jones to call or text, I readily agreed. But I had my doubts about Brenda Mumford and didn't want to be alone with her. "Will you or Anthony be there?" I asked.

"Both of us will be here unless there's a body to pick up."

Seeing as business was bad, that wouldn't be likely. I hung up, explained where I was going to Abuela, and she followed me out. "About Nalissa," she began.

"Yes?"

"Her intentions are noble, but there's no fuzziness or blurred lines between the magenta and bold red that define her most. She's intent on revealing big truths in an effort to help society but doesn't yet possess the ability to understand what truths aren't meant to be pursued or brought to light by her. In many ways, it makes her a great reporter, but it also makes her dangerous to others, even when she doesn't mean to be."

As usual with Abuela Luci's insights, there was a lot to process.

I dropped off Tito (who was barking mad about leaving Alondra right when she was fighting off her twin sister) at my house and drove to River's Bend Funeral Home, all the while thinking about what Abuela had said.

I knocked on the embalming room's back door, and Brenda answered. We hadn't seen each other since the day we found the picture of Tilly and Bonnie, and our exchanged pleasantries were stilted. Neither of us knew what to say. I looked around, surprised to see the embalmed body of a young male on the metal table next to Bonnie's. I cleared my throat and asked. "Um, where are Pappa and Anthony?"

"Oh. He called you to tell you they had to pick up a body, but you didn't answer. They left not two minutes ago." My eyes widened. A third body? Business was picking up for Pappa. Maybe the adage was true, that any publicity was good publicity. "But I really only needed to talk to you," Brenda continued. She walked toward Bonnie, and I followed, noting that she wasn't carrying a purse, and she was wearing form-fitting jeans and a white blouse, neither of which seemed to be hiding a gun, only a phone in her back pocket.

She stared down at Bonnie Crawford for a long time. It was all so awkward. I didn't know Brenda well, but it was clear she was struggling with her feelings. Pappa would probably know what to say. "Would you prefer to be alone?" I asked in a respectful tone.

"No. I'm okay." She released a long, tired breath. "It will take years of therapy to sort this out, and I already had years of therapy to deal with my childhood. But I find that I loved this woman, my aunt, even though she deceived me. Is that crazy?"

I considered it. "Maybe you understand her on some level. And maybe that helps you separate your memories of her from the hard facts you recently learned."

"Maybe…" She tilted her head slightly and studied Bonnie once more. "Things never quite added up when this woman, who I thought was my mom, came back from that trip to New York. But she explained she suffered some brain trauma in the accident, and that it was hard on her and she didn't want to talk about it, which made sense. I guess a part of me was always waiting for a shoe to drop, though."

She blew out a breath. "Detectives think they've pieced together what happened twelve years ago. It seems Tilly and Bonnie's last foster parents left them a small, out of the way property. Bonnie's friends say she had been a victim of domestic abuse for years and had finally separated from her husband, but she had trouble finding work that paid well. My mom wanted to sell the property, even though it wasn't worth much, but Bonnie hoped to convince her to let her have it. No one ever saw Bonnie again after she left to pick up my mom at the airport, but a truck driver called the police that night, saying he watched as a car swerved to avoid another, lost control, and went over a cliff, ending up in a lake. The car, Bonnie's old Pontiac, was found with what they were sure was her body in the driver's seat. They laid her to rest. But police now believe that my mom was the one who was driving and died, and when Bonnie resurfaced, she saw a chance at a new life."

She shook her head in disbelief. "Twelve years ago, this woman here took my mom's place, and the first thing she did was transfer almost all my mom's wealth over to me. It made me think she was sincere in turning over a new leaf. I don't know how much money she kept, but it couldn't have been much because she lived so simply. She paid for her small cottage in St. Anne's Hill with her mayor's salary, and before that, she rented a room. Looking back, I can see Bonnie here was only looking to start a new life. And that she had probably been screwed over by my real mom, too, during her life, because that's what my mom did. Bonnie Crawford just wanted a fresh start, and I think she finally became the person she'd always wished she could be."

She looked at me, expecting a response, and I searched for something sincere but neutral to say. It didn't seem like she wanted platitudes. "It must've been extremely difficult to step into another person's shoes. She must've wanted a new life very badly."

She nodded and looked down again. "She made plenty of mistakes. I even caught her starting her signature with a "B" a few times, but she said it was because I was on her mind, and my name starts with a "B". There was always a plausible explanation, and she mentioned brain trauma whenever she messed up in big ways, so I pushed my strange doubts aside." She smiled a little. "That's why I suggested you to Pappa. You looked at an old photograph and caught that slight difference in the mouth that made Tilly look mean, and Bonnie look kind. It was one of those things that nagged at me somewhere in the back of my mind."

Silence fell over us as Brenda continued to look thoughtful, and I tried to imagine what she was going through. "I'm sorry," she finally said. "I asked you here because detectives showed me a picture of Bonnie from just before she took my mom's place. Brenda dug out her phone and motioned me over. "See?" she asked and showed me the picture. I nodded. The hairstyle was different, parted in the middle instead of the side. "I think you should style it like this because it's what Bonnie preferred. I'll send it over to you.".

When she left, I took out my phone to get a more careful look at the picture she sent and saw I had missed calls and texts from Nalissa.

My heart began thudding so fast, and so hard, I became lightheaded and had to sit down. I quickly scrolled through everything, eager to get past her excuses until I read she had been mugged, and her phone had been stolen. It had taken her all this time to text me because she had to file a police report, claim a new phone, and download everything from her cloud.

My mind began to race, wondering if the pictures she had taken of my mom had anything to do with her phone being stolen, but I stopped myself. Nalissa was likely investigating other things, too, and nothing could be gained from speculation.

I zoomed into the picture of the framed collage on the wall above the table in the Carlsons' living room and looked for pictures of my parents, getting more and more lightheaded from anticipation by the moment. Until a notary's signature, and the name of a Dayton-based law firm brought my search to a sudden halt. They were under a snippet titled, "The first document we ever signed together," which was juxtaposed with "The most important document we'll ever sign." The first was a commercial lease, the second their marriage certificate. Both were signed by this notary.

An accomplice, just like in the telenovela…?

I turned to the desk in the corner. A folder was lying on top. Anthony had been researching the legal ramifications of the mayor's prepaid plan, and I hoped it was in the folder. I opened it, walked over to the light, caught Tilly's name, searched for the notary's signature, and tapped on it triumphantly.

"What are you doing?" a familiar voice asked.

Tessa Baker was standing not four feet away, watching me with wide, fearful eyes. I had been so eager to look at the pictures on my phone that I hadn't locked the door behind Brenda when she left.

My gaze slipped to her soft-soled shoes as I placed myself between the new corpse's head and Tessa. I tried to smile, but I'm not good at faking smiles. My mouth and nose always ended up looking like something smelled. "I'm going over the mayor's prepaid contract, to see if she made any other requests."

Her right hand trembled as it slipped into her purse. I took a furtive glance at the embalmed corpse in front of me to see if there was a tool to defend myself with lying there. "I saw what you were doing," she said. "Your finger was tapping *my* name."

I swallowed. "I was reviewing the mayor's last wishes. I didn't realize my finger was on your name."

"You're sneaky, Angie Gomez," she said, her breath now quick and shallow. "I don't like that." She lifted a small gun out of her purse and pointed it at me. Her hand was still shaking. "Put your phone down and your hands up," she commanded, and I complied. Strangely enough, I felt calm. The worst thing that could happen to me had already happened to me years before. Nothing else could compare.

Tessa watched me unblinkingly. "Ever since you figured out who the mayor really was, I realized you tricked me into helping you put it all together. I had to then spread the story like everyone would expect me to, and act shocked, so no one would suspect me, but now I can't get away from it! When Brenda said she'd be talking to you tonight, I decided to come in after she left. To see your reaction. Check if you were afraid to be alone with me. And here you were, tapping *my* name. How did you figure out it was me? What did I *say*?"

She was frantic and desperate. It made me think that even though she had shot and killed before, it wasn't something she had relished doing. She was in over her head, and her mental health had likely been deteriorating ever since the mayor's real identity came out. If I used her reluctance to kill me to keep her talking, maybe I could buy time to figure a way out of this. "It wasn't anything you said. It was something Brenda said, and from there, things clicked."

"What did Brenda say?" she asked, looking alarmed. Her entire body was shaking now.

"Only that Bonnie made little mistakes at first," I spoke as if we were gossiping, and not like I had a gun pointed at my heart. "Like starting to sign her name with a B, but that she would explain it away as brain trauma from the accident. But then I saw your signature and title on a commercial lease for someone else, as a notary and paralegal for Brenda Mumford's husband's law firm, and I wondered if that's how you and the mayor had met when she began transferring her wealth to Brenda, and if you caught mistakes, too. You also must've noticed the difference in signatures when looking at both old and new documents." I paused and took a deep breath, knowing my next comment would either keep her talking or set her off. "Is that how you figured it out? Did she make too many mistakes?" I asked in a conversational tone.

She closed her eyes a moment, and when she opened them again, she looked pained. "You're a smart girl, Angie. Your Grandma Nydia was right."

That threw me. "You know my Grandma Nydia?" I repeated.

Tessa smiled. "I met her once when she was visiting you from Puerto Rico. She said it was a shame you wasted that mind of yours by studying art. You could've been secretary of state, she said."

"Maybe I should've been a detective," I said and shrugged to cover I was lowering my hands a little. "Maybe you should've been one, too. When did you first suspect Tilly Sandberg was an impostor?"

Her eyes rolled to the side as if she were thinking about it, and I lowered my arms a tiny bit more. "I noticed the signatures weren't anything alike right away, and her explanation about brain trauma made sense, and I accepted it, but as a chief paralegal and a notary, I had to be thorough, and I asked her to bring in a note from a neurologist. But she never did. She always had an excuse, and she began to look nervous. I had seen enough in my career to know she was hiding something, but never in a million years would I have guessed what it was. Then, one day, she signed "Bonnie Crawford". When she caught it, she became agitated and said she had been thinking about an old friend. When she left, I looked up the name Bonnie Crawford, not sure what I was looking for, and scrolled through a few pages of women with that name until I found a news article from a small-town paper in New York about how a woman named Bonnie Crawford had died and divers had pulled her body from a lake. A picture of her, from her driver's license, accompanied the article. To say I was shocked is an understatement." Her eyes cleared and refocused on me. She raised the hand holding the gun a few inches, and it again began to shake.

"And you decided to help her?" I asked, deciding "help" was a safer word than "blackmail."

She nodded sadly. "I did. Because she told me about years and years of abuse, at the orphanage, from Tilly, and then her husband, and I understood. About feeling taken advantage of and not being valued. We became close, and she came to me often for advice on how to maintain the fiction. And all I asked in return was that she give me the money to buy the house in the Oregon District and fully renovate it. It had been my grandparents' home, and all my best memories were there. Memories of being valued. All I wanted were good memories, and to retire from a job where I wasn't valued enough." Her voice was as sweet as ever, and it was difficult to believe she was a murderer.

"Why did you do it? Why—why did you shoot her?"

She shook her head, looking desperately sad and haunted. "Because Jim Russo thought Tilly was loaded and was pressuring her to give money to his organization. Guilt over deceiving Brenda was starting to weigh heavily on Bonnie, and his pressure pushed her over the edge. She was going to confess. I couldn't let her do that. She was going to drag me down with her. After all the help I'd given her, and the little I'd asked for in return, she was only thinking about herself and not valuing my life and what would become of it. Not valuing our friendship. Like she'd complained everyone had always done to her." She steadied her right hand with her left and aimed the gun at my heart once more, looking determined. The embalming table was my only hope, but my palms were still a few inches above it.

"What were her last words?" I asked, needing to know.

"I told her that Bonnie was dead, that she was Tilly now, and that she had to accept it. She said, 'Bonnie *is* dead,' but I saw I could tell it didn't mean the same thing to her that it meant to me. I was done talking. And I'm done talking now. I don't want to do this. Pappa will have figured out there was no dead body to pick up by now."

She aimed her gun. I heard it click.

With a cry for strength, I shoved the embalming table at Tessa with all my might, but instead of sliding, the table tipped over, corpse and all, and my miscalculation sent me over with it. Tessa didn't move in time and got knocked over. I landed on top of the dead man, who was partially on top of Tessa, and his last words, "*Remember. Shell,*" croaked in my head. The gun fell and discharged, and someone burst through the door calling, "Angie!" In the distance, sirens screamed.

An instant later, I found myself lifted off the corpse and embraced by Lieutenant Brian Mahoney, who cursed softly into my hair.

"Is she dead?" I asked against his shoulder. I didn't want her to be. Not by my hand.

"She's knocked out but breathing. Hold on." He let me go, and pried the corpse off Tessa's lower half, checked her pulse, and then rolled her over and handcuffed her.

He came back and gently tipped my chin up with his thumb to study me. "Are you okay?"

"Yes. How did you know to come here?"

"Anthony called 911 to say they were tricked into leaving you alone with Brenda Mumford, and he was afraid for you. He thought she might have gotten someone to make the false call. But we had already zeroed in on Tessa Baker, and detectives hadn't found her at home earlier in the evening, so they called all units to come here, in case. I was at my house, basically across the street from the cemetery, and ran over."

The sound of sirens drew closer. I took a step back and crossed my arms. "I asked you if it was Tessa that night at the station. You became exasperated with me and made me think I was silly for asking."

The corner of his mouth lifted. "I never become exasperated, but I do remember you weren't taking my warnings seriously about being careful with people, including Tessa Baker. I was frustrated."

"So, she was a suspect, and you placed me in harm's way by not telling me."

"Tessa wasn't even a person of interest. But when we went back twelve years on everyone close to Bonnie, we found an unexplained financial windfall for Tessa Baker."

I smiled. "You went back twelve years because of my missing birthmark discovery."

He smiled, too. "We'd have gotten there eventually." Sirens, car doors, and voices were just beyond the door.

"I helped."

"And almost got yourself killed."

"I was resourceful."

His gaze became serious. "You were. And I'm relieved. If anything had happened to you—" He shook his head. "This has got to stop."

"What?" I asked, confused because I wasn't sure if he was talking to me or himself. He gave me a look and turned to meet the officers walking in.

An hour later, after I'd told my story, in detail, countless times, Pappa, Anthony, and I were finally alone.

"Tessa Baker." Pappa whistled low. "I didn't have her on my bingo card, did either of you?"

I flashed back to the night I asked Mahoney if Tessa was a suspect. "No. Not seriously, at least. She seemed so harmless. But boy, did she have a lot of pent-up grievances!"

Pappa nodded sagely. "Gotta watch out for those who keep everything bottled up inside. They either explode or implode, and it's never pretty."

Anthony glanced at me. "Well, everyone was on my bingo card. Which is why I'm so sorry we left you alone with Brenda, even if she didn't end up being the murderer. We'll do better next time."

"Next time?" Pappa asked.

Anthony motioned with his head to the new body, and we congregated around it. "You broke his nose," he said.

"He fell on Tessa's bony hip. Contouring will make it look good as new." I paused then, because I'd heard the man's last words, and they were odd. "What's, um, what's his name?"

"Ronnie Martin," Pappa said on a soft sigh. I gave him a questioning look because he seemed especially sad. "Suicide," he explained.

I took a deep breath and slowly let it out. "I didn't mean to, but my face landed on top of the back of his head, and I heard his last words."

Pappa shook his head. "No, don't tell us. Too disrespectful to know what he was thinking in his last moments."

"Actually," Anthony began, and the hesitation in his voice made us both look at him. "It was *ruled* a suicide. By hanging. But his mother and fiancée don't buy it. They called us because they're desperate, and they read about how Angie's observation helped with the mayor's murder case. They're hoping she sees something." He turned to me. "And I was hoping you hear something."

Pappa nodded at me encouragingly, and his permission was all I needed. "Ronnie Martin's last words were '*Remember. Shell*' in a strangled voice."

They were quiet as they let those words sink in.

"Shell," Pappa repeated after a while. "Like short for Shelley, or Sheldon, or Michelle, maybe."

"It's definitely a start," Anthony said, his eyes bright.

Pappa put a hand on my shoulder, then. "Wait. What about your parents, Angie? Did you finally hear from Nalissa?"

"Yes, and she sent the pictures. Lillian Carlson was the person sitting next to my mom at dinner that night. My dad was on her other side. I don't know what it means, or how it all fits together, but I have some ideas..." And now we had Ronnie to look into, too.

I was so anxious to get started, my heart felt like it was throbbing in my throat as if I had regurgitated it and then swallowed it again. I had to find a way to calm down enough to think things through this time. I couldn't let my parents down by messing up. And though I was prepared to make enemies, I had to try to avoid getting good people, like Maddie Lentil, involved.

"Just remember three heads are better than one," Anthony said as if he'd read my thoughts.

I smiled at him gratefully. "What did you say to Ronnie Martin's family?"

"I said I knew you'd try, and then I offered them a discount."

"A discount?" I repeated.

"Discounts for murders…" Pappa said thoughtfully before nodding once, decisively. "A way to help people financially during a difficult time."

"And a good way to attract business."

"*And*… a good way to find murders to investigate," I added, my pulse speeding up at the thought of using my gift to help others find justice.

WORD GAMES

ANGIE GOMEZ COZY MURDER MYSTERY, BOOK 2

"Angie!" Anthony suddenly exclaimed, his eyes as bright as a lightbulb. "What if you can also feel a corpse's last feeling, or smell the last thing they smelled, too?"

We all stared down at Ronnie Martin's body. "In the name of solving another case," Papa prodded.

"In the name of solving another case," I repeated, staring at Ronnie's broken nose. I took in a deep breath and let it out. Then another. On the third, Anthony quickly leaned down and took a sniff into the corpse's nose.

"See?" He tried to smile through his cringe. "Nothing to it."

I rolled my eyes at him, but his gambit worked. If Anthony could do it merely to encourage me, I could do it to have a better chance at solving a case. Gingerly, I leaned down and took a quick sniff in the area around his nose and sprung right back up. "Nothing!" I exclaimed with a squeak.

"How about feel what he feels?" Pappa asked. I studied the body on the embalming table. "Maybe if you put your heart next to his," he suggested.

I nodded once, squared my shoulders, and leaned over Ronnie, touching my heart to his as I closed my eyes. At first, nothing. Then, the sound of metal slamming against metal.

I opened my eyes. Abuela was standing at the door. "Are we literally embracing death now, Angie?" She was striving for humor, but her eyes were cloudy, and the lines around her mouth were tight. Fear. It used to show up whenever my dad would go on a trip or when he was acting dicey. She strove for humor because she didn't want me to stop living my life, and she had learned that interfering led nowhere. But it didn't mean she didn't feel, and I wondered what I could do to wipe the clouds from her eyes and lines from her face.

"I, uh, was checking for a heartbeat," I explained. Anthony rolled his eyes.

Abuela raised an eyebrow. "A heartbeat?"

"I once saw a report on how a young woman in Wyoming was declared dead but was still alive. I wanted to make sure," I explained, gently pushing off Ronnie and then smoothing the white blanket covering him.

Abuela shrugged. "You third cousin twice removed, Monchito, got up during the middle of his wake and asked for a bottle of Ron cañita. We gave it to him because we were too shocked to refuse, but his liver apparently couldn't handle much more because that last drop was what killed him."

I gave her a look. "Who brings moonshine rum to a funeral service?"

"We all did. We were going to drink a toast because that's what Monchito would have wanted."

Silence. The clouds and lines were still there. Anthony and Pappa were staring at the machete. Abuela was studying Ronnie. "What happened to him?" she asked, her eyes suddenly narrowed.

Anthony cleared his throat. "Apparent suicide."

Abuela tilted her head. "It's possible. His aura is greatly troubled."

My jaw dropped. "His aura? Dead people have auras?"

"Only when they leave during great, emotional trauma. The turmoil leaves energy behind."

"Why hadn't you told me this before? It's fascinating. You love being fascinating!"

"It's only recently you seem to believe." She gave me a look, and again, I caught a sense of her both being curious and not wanting to know because she didn't want to interfere. She was afraid to interfere. Now that I believed fully believed in magical Gomez powers, I could see where she was coming from.

Available in Paperback and eBook from Your Favorite Bookstore or Online Retailer

ABOUT THE AUTHOR

Ines Saint was born in Zaragoza, Spain and grew up with one foot on an island of Puerto Rico and the other in the States. She's bilingual and bicultural and has spent the last eighteen years raising her fun, inspiring boys and sharing her life with her husband/best friend/biggest fan. Her greatest joys are spending quality time with family and close friends, traveling, reading feel-good historical fiction, hiking, and snuggling next to her dog, Hobbit.

www.inessaint.com

 twitter.com/Ines%20Saint

 instagram.com/InesSaintBooks